# MESSAGES AND OTHER STORIES

Roger,

I hope you will enjoy my stories. I have been interested by your poetic form.

Warm regards,

Peter

# MESSAGES

## AND OTHER STORIES

Peter Dawson

First published in 2011 on behalf of the author by
Scotforth Books, Carnegie House,
Chatsworth Road, Lancaster LA1 4SL

ISBN 13: 978-1-904244-66-0

Printed in the UK by Blissets, London

# CONTENTS

*Writing is not about something,*
*it is that something itself.*

*Samuel Beckett*

The author was for ten years the headmaster of an Inner London mixed comprehensive school for 2000 pupils. His account of that was a best-seller in 1981. He then became general secretary of the Professional Association of Teachers and successfully achieved its recognition in negotiating the pay and conditions of service of teachers. He was appointed a UK delegate to the economic and social committee of the European Community in Brussels. He was made an OBE, then sat for twelve years as a lay member of the employment appeal tribunal, a branch of the high court, and became its official historian. For many years he was a regular newspaper columnist on issues in education. He is an ordained minister of the Methodist Church. This book is his first work of fiction.

## BY THE SAME AUTHOR

*Making a Comprehensive Work:*
*The Road from Bomb Alley* (Blackwell)

*Teachers and Teaching* (Blackwell)

*Why Preach?* (Foundery Press)

*A Short History of the Employment Appeal Tribunal*
(Moorley's Publishing)

# MESSAGES

St Bride's Church is just off Fleet Street. It was once the parish church of the newspaper industry, before the great printing houses departed to escape the grip of the old print unions. St Bride's steeple, with its five octagonal stages, has been compared to an elaborate wedding cake. St Bride's is the tallest of the many churches designed by Christopher Wren after the Great Fire had gutted the City. Three and a half centuries later, St Bride's provides a quiet retreat from the noise and traffic fumes of Fleet Street; a place to which people come who are wearied by the pressures of everyday life. There is a notice board in the church upon which people place prayer requests and messages asking for help.

As was his custom most mornings, a gaunt old man entered St Bride's and shuffled towards the board. He tried to read those messages that were sufficiently legible for his bloodshot eyes. 'Please do something about my husband's drinking', said one. 'Chloe, my sad sister', said another, without elaboration. 'God, why do you allow kids to be born crippled?', objected one contributor. 'Good question', muttered the old man to himself. He twisted his head to read a longer statement that was askew on the board, but soon gave up, realizing it was in a foreign language. He thought of the man from some place in Europe who used to sleep near him under the bridge beside the underground station at Charing Cross. One morning he had been found dead. Hardly anybody noticed.

The man's attention was caught by something written on a piece of paper that was the top half of a page torn from a telephone directory. Superimposed on the print, in bold black capitals, written with a felt-tipped pen, were a dozen words: 'Please help me find my son who is lost in this city.' It annoyed him that anyone should have torn up what he regarded as an important publication. His wandering mind went back to his childhood when, on Friday afternoons, his teacher would read *Treasure Island* to the class. One of Long John Silver's men had torn a page from a Bible to draw a black spot on it and been warned by the one-legged pirate that he was doomed for doing that. The old man knew he was doomed. He knew he stank, but was past caring.

It was warm in the church. That's why he came most days, as autumn gave way to winter and the bite of cold winds tormented the bones of his skeletal frame. He found himself a comfortable corner in a pew behind a stone column, and settled down. Reaching into the pocket of his tattered overcoat, he took out the cold remains of a hamburger he had retrieved from a bin. The purchaser had obviously gone off it, or lost his appetite, after a couple of bites. The man sniffed it, like a dog exploring a lamp post, then sank his teeth into it. He had intended taking his time eating it, and maybe keep a morsel for later, but he had not for a long time been able to exercise much self-control. He stuffed the food in his mouth, shoving it in with filthy fingers so that his cheeks bulged. He coughed a little as he swallowed his breakfast, then sank back exhausted. Soon, overcome by warmth and the comfort of having something to eat, he fell asleep.

The vicar entered the church from his vestry to collect the items pinned to the board. His lined face was that of someone who shared many people's burdens; the slight droop of his shoulders gave the same impression. But the glint in his eye, and something about his mouth, suggested that his sense of humour had not left him. As he plucked the pieces of paper from the board, his hand hesitated over the one torn from a telephone directory. Sighing, with just a hint of disapproval, he added it to the rest.

Back at his desk, the man of God laid the scraps of paper out and read each message with care. Then he offered a prayer: 'Lord, you know who wrote these things, and why. Please do what you know, as I do not, what is best for them.' Then, with a wry smile, based on his long experience of dealing with the recipient of his prayers, he added: 'If there's anything you want me to do, show me. But please, not too difficult.'

As he collected the scraps to deposit them in his bin, the piece from a telephone directory fluttered to the floor under his chair. It lay there, unnoticed, all day. At evening, when the cleaner came, she picked it up and placed it carefully in the centre of the vicar's desk. Some believe that, through such small gestures, divine intervention in the affairs of men and women advances.

Next morning, the old tramp pulled open the church door and once more made his way to the board where messages were displayed. He did not know why he did this every time he came but he had long ago given up trying to work out why he did what he did. On the streets, he simply wandered from place to place each day, hoping something would turn up. Charles Dickens, he recalled, had created a character with the same approach to life. But the old man's appetite for reading had died with his appetite for life. He didn't expect to last another winter. Who cared?

The vicar observed the man standing at the board. He thought there must be a reason why he came almost every day and made a habit of reading the messages. Was he hoping for one having to do with his taking to the streets? Was something going on beyond the vicar's understanding? It wouldn't be the first time. He thought: 'God moves in a mysterious way his wonders to perform.' That line, written by William Cowper in the eighteenth century, had sometimes impelled the vicar when he had not much idea what he was supposed to be doing in dealing with the disparate human needs that arrived at his door.

As the tramp's gaze passed over the notice board, his attention was once again aroused by a piece of paper torn from a telephone directory. The message, again written in bold black capitals over the directory text, was partly obscured by another piece of paper. All he could see was: 'Please bring …' Bring what? Peace to the world? Some hopes. He was too tired to reach out and see what someone was yearning for. Soon, he was fast asleep in his usual place.

The vicar reappeared and collected the items on the board. Sitting at his desk with the morning's collection of slips in his hand, he saw the one from yesterday that had been carefully left for his attention. The upper edge of the new piece of paper fitted the lower edge of yesterday's. It was the bottom half of the same page. Putting the two scraps of paper together, the vicar sat staring at the complete request for some time: 'Please help me find my son who is lost in this city. Please bring James home.'

The vicar spent a good deal of the day, between his other duties, watching out for visitors to the notice board. His vigilance was rewarded in the early evening when he had almost given up and his mind had begun to turn to his evening engagements. Thoughts of them fled his mind as a woman approached the board with a piece of paper in her hand that had clearly come from a cannibalized telephone directory. She took a drawing pin from the box below the board and reached out to post up her message. As she did so, she felt a hand gently touching her shoulder. Turning, she looked at the vicar questioningly. He said, 'I think you're looking for James, aren't you?'

Jane Burton was in her fifties, well dressed and confident in manner and speech, but manifestly bewildered at the turn of events. Sitting in the vestry, speaking of her search for her son, she said, 'James had everything to live for. Why did he give it all up?' The vicar responded by referring to her messages posted on the board. 'Tell me', he said, 'why have you been putting up bits of a telephone directory? It's a rather odd thing to do.'

Jane Burton smiled. Her demeanour softened as she spoke of her son. 'James worked in the telecommunications industry on the engineering side', she said. 'He has a first from Imperial', she said, with pride in her voice, 'I thought he might be drawn to pages from a telephone directory. He was always insisting that there wouldn't be any such publications but for those like him who designed the communications network.' A while later, the vicar's visitor prepared to leave, after he had invited her to return at the same time next day, when he might have something to report. 'You make me think there's hope', she said. 'Always there is hope', came the confident reply.

The vicar was restless that night. He did not feel confident. Would his suspicion prove justified? And if it was, how should he handle things tomorrow? He lay in bed in the dark, looking out at the night sky through the dormer window of his bedroom. The stars were bright in their heavenly places. 'I suppose', he said, looking out upon God's unfathomable creation, 'I suppose you know what you're doing, giving me pieces of a telephone directory to fit together. For heaven's sake, what next?' He had a very informal relationship with the object of his thoughts. From the bedroom shadows there came no divine words of guidance. But, as the vicar settled down to sleep, having unloaded on the Almighty, he felt at peace.

Next morning, the tramp was later than usual and looked even more gaunt and tired than before. He was disappointed to find no messages on the board, though he couldn't think why. He made to shuffle off into his usual corner, but heard a movement close behind. 'Were you looking for a message?', asked the vicar, who had just emptied the board. The man made no reply. He drew his coat around him in a defensive gesture. His eyes were wary, but lit up at the next question: 'Would you like a nice hot mug of tea?' The offer was irresistible.

Sitting in the warm vestry, drinking tea and munching digestive biscuits, the man thought to himself that this particular day was turning out well after a late start. 'Tell me about yourself', said the vicar. Observing the man close up, he realized that the appearance of old age was misleading. Life on the streets of London had taken a heavy toll on his wellbeing. The long, straggly hair, sunken eyes and dirt-encrusted features obscured a young man's face. The vicar asked the question he always did when talking to someone who was struggling and possibly on the brink of despair: 'What's your story?'

Guardedly, the man responded. He came from a good home. He had qualifications in electrical engineering and good career prospects until things went wrong in his private life. He just walked away and took to the streets. He had said things, terrible things, unforgivable things, to those at home. He could never go back. 'Nothing', said the vicar, 'is unforgivable. Absolutely nothing.' The man shook his head in disbelief. His name was James and he designed telecommunications systems. 'Without people like me', he asserted, 'telephone directories would be just scrap paper.' The vicar said, 'If you will come with me, you can have a bath and some fresh clothes, then some hot food and a good sleep in a comfortable bed. After that, we'll come back here. There's someone I want you to meet.'

# FALLING STAR

At the end of the geography lesson, the setting of homework brought groans from the year five class. The teacher said, 'It's no good groaning. You've got your exams this year. So homework is for your own good. It shows I love you.' There was good-natured laughter round the room. 'You are not expected to like it, you are expected to do it', said Roderick Sheringham.

Stephen Grice, who clearly had a promising career as an entertainer awaiting him when he left school, was acknowledged as a brilliant mimic of the teacher who regularly uttered this maxim. One hand tucked in his belt, the other clutching a lapel, rocking back and forth on his feet, he would reduce onlookers to helpless laughter as he delivered his star performance as the teacher known as 'Rocky' Sheringham. 'You are not', he would declare, echoing the teacher's tone of voice, 'expected to like it. You are expected to do it.' The boy's skill as a mimic was admired throughout the school.

Roderick Sheringham, observed by a group of boys in company with his wife at prizegiving, was the subject of comment: 'Fancy having to live with him'. The possibility that he was a normal human being at home was hard to imagine. Who was the boss on the domestic front? Did his wife tell him, when he complained that he was too tired to mow the lawn: 'You're not expected to like it. You're expected to do it.' Perhaps that was where he had got his favourite injunction from.

The idiosyncrasies of the staff had been one of the glories of this seventeenth century greycoat grammar school for boys down the years. They remained so as the 1950s unfolded. Roderick had taught there before his time as a tank commander in North Africa during the war against Hitler and had returned there after demobilization. He was a fine teacher and not at all concerned that one of the boys was, as he knew, able to do a perfect imitation of him. 'My dear chap', he once told a young man new to the profession who seemed to be worried about it, 'when they start to amuse themselves by emulating you, it shows you have made your mark. We teachers are all actors, you know. The classroom is a theatre in which we perform.'

He was fond of telling his classes in a suitably theatrical manner how he had chased Rommel across the Sahara. Those he taught enjoyed this and looked for opportunities to distract him from what he intended to teach by asking about his wartime adventures. Their ability to invent questions with that in mind sometimes showed considerable ingenuity. Even the treeless plains of the South American savannah could be turned to advantage. 'Sir, don't they have a desert like the Sahara in South America then?', asked Stephen Grice, an innocent expression of genuine inquiry on his face. 'No, Grice, and stop trying to change the subject', came the reply. 'But, sir', said the boy, not yet ready to give up, 'how would your tank squadron have operated if the terrain in Africa had been savannah?' 'It would have been a lot easier. Desert warfare is a grim business', came the reply. 'Why's that, sir', came a voice from the back. The whole class smiled. They were pretty sure that a point of no return had been reached. There was no way of bringing the subject of the lesson back to South America in face of such an appetizing question. Desert battle tactics took over. Well, it *was* Friday.

'Much homework for the weekend?', asked his mother as Stephen arrived home from school. 'Loads', came the reply. 'Don't look so glum', said Jane Grice, 'you must expect it if you want to make anything of yourself. You may not like it but you must just get on and do it.' 'You sound just like Rocky', replied her son.

Stephen was a very bright lad. By his academic performance, he had always retained his place in the top stream without difficulty. Only his prankishness kept him from being a model pupil although, even in this regard, there were teachers who felt he brought a certain commendable excitement to the classroom. His most ingenious joke had been the invention, with the assistance of a couple of his friends, of a phantom physics pupil. That had been done at the expense of a somewhat naïve young newcomer to the staff who had yet to discover that, in a highly selective grammar school, some of those sitting in the desks were cleverer than those who stood at the blackboard.

Stephen Grice and his partners in crime acquired a new exercise book, entered the name J. Robinson on the cover, and the subject, physics, wrote up the latest homework and handed it in for marking. Next lesson, the tenderfoot teacher handed out the books he had marked and called for Robinson to receive his. 'He's new', said Stephen Grice, 'and he's away today. I'll take his book for him, sir.'

Throughout the term, the same pattern was repeated, with members of the miscreant trio offering an amazing variety of explanations for Robinson's non-appearance. He seemed to have a talent for physics, although the teacher commented once or twice on his appalling handwriting, which seemed to have no consistent style. 'I've never seen writing quite like Robinson's,' the teacher observed on one occasion. 'I think he was dropped on his head as a baby, sir', opined Stephen Grice, 'he's a clever chap but a bit unco-ordinated.' The teacher thought to himself that he looked forward to meeting this Robinson when he had got over the unfortunate series of mishaps and maladies of which he had been victim since joining the school.

All was revealed when end-of-term reports were due to be written and the young teacher began to seek the whereabouts of the report for Robinson of 5A. 'There is no Robinson in 5A', said George Tate, mathematician and staffroom tipster, from behind his copy of 'Sporting Life'. 'But there must be', came the reply, 'I've got a whole line of marks for him in my mark book.' But other staff supported George. Stanley Cranmer, classicist, after some thought about the membership of 5A, observed dryly: 'It's Grice. He'll be behind it.'

Once he moved up into the sixth form, the young man in question took his A level studies in English, geography and economics in his stride. In the last subject named, he developed an ability to see beyond the traditional Keynesian solution to problems and ask questions of an amazingly penetrative kind for one of his age. On occasions, he and his teacher became involved in exchanges that left the rest of the class behind.

Discussing the sixth former in question at morning break one day, Gerald Plant, economist, declared: 'Young Grice is cleverer than me, and I suspect he is aware of it. I'll be surprised if he doesn't get an Oxbridge place. I wish I could persuade him to go for PPE but there's no prizing him away from geography.' James Cumberland, an English specialist from one of the newer universities who was no respecter of the old guard said, 'It's not the subject, old chap, it's the teacher.' Fortuitously, the bell went for the end of break.

When the school's star pupil began to behave strangely, Roderick Sheringham was the first to notice. At the outset, Stephen's handwriting began to deteriorate. It became worse than that of the phantom physicist he had once invented. Then, one morning, he was unable to handle a simple question about ocean currents. His words did not make sense. 'Steve must have gone pubbing last night', said a member of the class, making a joke of the situation. The moment quickly passed and the lesson proceeded, but the teacher was worried. He wondered if others who taught the boy had noticed anything.

'There's something wrong with Grice', said Roderick Sheringham in the staff room. 'It's his sense of humour', observed George Tate, 'I knew it would get him into trouble one day.' But the trouble that engulfed the young man in question left little room for humour among those who cared about him. The diagnosis was progressive muscular atrophy, the outcome certain.

Roderick went to see his star pupil who had shone so brightly in the school firmament. As he sat in the hospital waiting area, he found himself in company with Stephen's devastated parents. They spoke of the awesome decision that had to be made. 'He wants the lung to be turned off', said his distraught mother. The teacher thought of the boy who had so skilfully led him to discuss desert battle tactics when he should have been teaching geography. 'If he has decided that's what he wants', said Roderick, 'he will find an opportunity to have his way.'

They stood over the young man's head as it protruded from the apparatus that was keeping him alive. He spoke only with difficulty, his determination to be heard etched on his wasted features. 'Hullo, sir', he whispered, 'you're just the person I need.' He paused, struggling for the strength to speak again. His teacher bent down and held his ear close to Stephen's mouth. 'Tell them', said Stephen, moving his eyes to look longingly at his parents, 'tell them to have me turned off.' The trace of a smile crossed his lips. 'Tell them', he said, 'that they're not expected to like it, but they must do it.'

# PERFORMANCE

With so much going on around him, James Seaton found it impossible to concentrate on the papers before him. He regretted leaving it until he was on the train to study them. On the other side of the table, two men were arguing about some kind of contract. Other business travellers were loudly pouring instructions into their mobiles.

As the train pulled out of Sheffield towards London, a young woman collapsed into the seat beside James and began to weep. He drew out the silk handkerchief that spilled from the breast pocket of his suit and offered it to the woman. She shook her head and, fetching paper tissue from her capacious bag, blew her nose trumpetingly.

She was a big person. That, it soon emerged, was precisely her problem. Taking out a mobile, she punched in a number and explained her distress to a friend. 'Steve's going to leave me', she said. With a mixture of anger and self-pity, she spelled out her predicament, her voice escalating from contralto to mezzo soprano. 'He says I'm too fat', she complained, 'and being with me is like living in the elephant house at the zoo.' There were more tears and further elephantine trumpeting as she held a tissue to her nose, then she said, 'He must be somewhere on this train. It's the one we always catch. I don't know what I'll do if I see him.'

A second drama was developing the other side of the table. 'We can't possibly agree to that', said the man immediately opposite James, 'there's not a hope in hell of our meeting the delivery date.' He had the purple face of a heavy drinker and big hands. His feet nudged James', searching for more space. He looked harassed. His companion, a dapper character with sharp features and shifty eyes responded: 'We don't need to mention that, for God's sake, let's just get the contract.' His companion shifted uneasily in this seat. 'It could all bloody end in tears', he asserted. There was a fresh outbreak of weeping beside James, as if to endorse what Big Hands had just said.

Across the aisle, a woman was talking to someone at home on her mobile. 'Hullo darlin', it's me. Are you up? Of course I woke you before I left. I did. I did. You must have dropped off again.' There was some kind of response, then, 'So you *are* up now. Right? Where are you then?' She turned to her companion. 'Reggie's in the kitchen eating toast', she reported. 'And the kids?', she asked, reverting to Reggie, 'Did you get them off to school?' The answer was clearly satisfactory and the woman's tone changed. 'Have a nice day, hunky', she said. The response evoked a giggle. 'Cheeky bugger', she said.

Leaning forward, pretending to look at his papers, James turned his head to glance at the woman. Her hair was blonde by adoption. She wore a bright red sweater and nail varnish to match. 'I bet they think we'll go mad today,' she said. There was a chuckle from her friend sitting beside her. 'They could be right', she declared, 'I've got my credit card with me. Jack took it off me after the last time but I got it back when we were on good terms again. He tried to get me to hand it over last night but gave up when Man United came on.' She paused. 'With him', she continued, 'everything stops for football. Including his little mind.' Both women laughed raucously. Blondie's friend was in a bright yellow dress. James thought the two women together looked like characters from a cartoon.

A man's voice behind James said, 'Did you see the programme on the Holocaust?' 'Of course', came the slightly irritable reply, 'how could either of us have missed it?' 'We have to forgive, you know', said the first voice. It was older and more patient than the first. 'Forgive? Never. Not ever', came the response. James could not resist turning round. The two men wore the black hats and long, curling sideburns of orthodox Jews. James had seen the Holocaust programme. It had brought back the memory of what his grandfather had told him about walking into Belsen at the end of the war. Grandfather had been one of an army detachment sent to handle the survivors of that place of death. 'It was like walking into the mouth of hell', James was told, 'They were like stick insects. The stink was overwhelming. Unforgivable.'

'Unforgivable!', declared James' tearful neighbour. She was on her mobile again, regaling another friend with an account of the collapse of her relationship with Steve. 'How could he treat me like that? He's inhuman!', she exclaimed. James thought that, in the record of man's inhumanity to man, this woman's experience would not make the history books. He took a closer look and saw that the woman had a very attractive face. The ancient Greeks would have thought her beautiful. Was it Aeschylus who wrote that a buxom woman had, of all women, the greater beauty? Greek art demonstrated that belief. But perhaps Steve was not into that.

As he was about to make an attempt to read the documents in front of him ready for his afternoon meeting, the distractions around James became Shakespearean with the arrival of a ticket collector who littered his conversation with quotations from the works of Britain's greatest playwright. When he was on duty, his poetic passage down the train was always eagerly awaited. He reached Big Hands who, handing over his ticket, asked aggressively, 'Where's the coffee trolley? There's supposed to be one on this train.' 'I have had a dream', the inspector patiently declared, 'past the wit of man to say what dream it was, but I think I saw a trolley.' As its approaching rattle sounded he declared, 'Once more unto the breach it comes,' and moved on down the train.

Elegantly formidable, a woman in her late thirties passed through the carriage from the first class end of the train. The Burberry lining of her raincoat, which hung open, denoted her social class, as she perhaps intended. She carried an expensive red leather briefcase. Conversation subsided as passengers' eyes followed her progress. She was a handsome woman but James thought he would not want to do business with her. What was it Francois Mitterand had said about Margaret Thatcher? That she had the mouth of Marilyn Monroe but the eyes of Caligula. When the woman had gone, red jumper said, 'I bet she's a bitch.' 'Yea', responded her companion, 'but a nice coat.'

As the train passed through Kilburn, there was the usual movement by some passengers to extract themselves from their seats and take up prime positions in the rush to disembark. Like greyhounds in the slips, thought James. At St Pancras, he joined the human flood heading for the underground. Passing through the station concourse, he thought he saw his tearful fellow-traveller locked in an embrace with a man.

In mid-afternoon, James left the place of his meeting in the City to make an early start home. At St Pancras, he went into a coffee shop. A back-packer in front of him in the queue for service was carefully counting the coins in his hand. James was suddenly taken back to his gap year between school and university, when he had travelled all round Europe with two of his friends. What adventures they had! The young man in front of him reached the counter and said, 'Coffee, please.' The girl serving asked, 'Large or small?' 'What's the difference?', asked the back-packer, checking once more the money he was holding. The girl raised her eyebrows and patiently explained. 'With large', she said, 'you get more coffee.'

Boarding his train, James spotted the weeping woman who had sat beside him that morning. Her eyes were shining. She was with the man he had seen embracing her in the station concourse earlier in the day. They were laughing happily as they found seats together. A couple passing along the carriage greeted them. 'Hullo, you two', said one, 'so you've made it up again. How many more times are you going to give us all the run around before the wedding?' Shining Eyes giggled. Her companion was built like a rugby union second row forward. James thought he had seen him play. He dwarfed his well-built wife-to-be. He laughed in response to the comment of the passing couple. He said,

'Rucking is part of our lifestyle. We're both built for it.'

Arriving home, James kissed his wife. 'What was the journey like this morning?', she asked, 'Did you manage to read those documents?' 'I didn't get much work done on the train', he replied, 'there was too much going on. It was like being at the theatre.' His wife said, 'I hope you've not forgotten that we're going to see that new revue, *Funny People,* at the playhouse tonight. The Yorkshire Post said it was terrific.' James said, 'It will have to be good to beat today's performance.'

# WEEKEND BREAK

*The following story had its genesis in a press report some years ago concerning a decision by a seaside resort to demolish its pier, which was in an advanced state of decay. What made the story unusual, and therefore worth the attention of the media in the silly season, was the method chosen. The pier was blown up. There was a picture of a local worthy pressing a button which set off the detonation.*

'It's time we got rid of it. It was built in the nineteen-twenties. It's beyond repair,' said Councillor Phillips. He had made his money in the demolition business and was never averse to having something knocked down. In the present case, the argument for demolition was strong. Estimates had shown that the cost of repairing Spraycombe pier would run to six figures while removing it would cost much less, however it were done. 'It's become a real eyesore and puts people off coming here', said Councillor Walker, whose wife worked at the tourist information office and had given him clear instructions to have what she called 'that decaying monstrosity' removed.

But there was a voice raised against. 'I can remember', said Agnes Choke, 'when bands played on it all summer, and there was dancing too.' Some of her council colleagues could indeed recall when this now large and florid lady, of smaller dimensions at the time, waltzed on the pier in its prime, which coincided with hers.

The proposal to demolish what remained of the pier was overwhelmingly carried but, once taken, left open the question of arrangements to have it done. It was at this point that the resort's director of leisure services, Henry Butler, rose to his feet after indicating to the chairman that he would like to speak. Councillor Brigden shifted uneasily in his seat. A former military man, George Brigden saw one of his principal duties on the council as being to resist the bright ideas of the leisure director. 'Too much of a young upstart for me', he would say, 'and too clever by half. Not really our sort of chap.' George had always felt put out by not being on the appointing committee for the post Henry occupied.

'If we have to demolish the old wreck, we must do it in style', said Henry Butler. He was looking at Councillor Brigden as he said this. The Councillor raised an eyebrow and pursed his lips, but thought that perhaps no double entendre had been intended. 'What we should do', the director continued, 'is arrange to have explosive charges set by experts, blow up the pier, and have the demolished superstructure removed by the same firm.' 'That sounds logical', said Councillor Phillips. Henry Butler became quite excited as he continued. 'What we should do', he said, 'is hold a competition to see who is to press the button to detonate the charges.'

The cacophony that greeted this suggestion was a mixture of excited approval and outraged disbelief. 'You cannot be serious', expostulated George Brigden, his face puce with rage. 'Oh, yes he can', said Florrie Simpson, a strong-minded matriarch at home and a force to be reckoned with throughout Spraycombe, which was quite a small town. Formidable Florrie, as she was known, had once been headmistress of the local grammar school for girls and she still reminded her hearers from time to time of the things she was never in the habit of putting up with from her gels. By implication, there was a good deal she wouldn't tolerate from anybody else either, including the likes of George Brigden. She had despised him ever since he had voted against giving land in the town for the building of a youth club. 'It'll only encourage thugs', he had declared, 'and that means most young people today.' 'It would give them a worthwhile place to go instead of daubing graffiti all over the place', Florrie had insisted. But the proposal was voted down and her opinion of Councillor Brigden had never recovered. He was quite undisturbed by this. 'The trouble with teachers', he had been known to say, 'is that they bear grudges. Did you know that one of Queen Florence's staff opposed a sixth former's appointment as a prefect because she had been a bit of a tearaway in the third form? How's that for harbouring a grudge, eh?' The strength of his feelings was no doubt in part due to the fact that his granddaughter was the girl concerned although, of course, he bore no grudge.

After a long and appropriately explosive discussion about how to proceed, the director of leisure was given the task of finding a suitable contractor to set charges at the pier and to remove the consequent debris. He was also asked to make arrangements for a competition of the kind he had suggested. As the council laid down no specifics as to the latter task, Henry Butler felt that he had a free hand.

Henry was a native of Spraycombe who, unlike many of that ilk, looked beyond the immediate locality in his thinking. That being so, he had an idea to advertise the competition to which the council had agreed in neighbouring seaside resorts. After a while, he became more ambitious and planned to extend it to resorts throughout England. Discussing his plans over a drink with a fellow Rotarian as they gathered for their fortnightly lunch, one of them said, 'Why limit yourself to seaside towns? I reckon some big city folk might enjoy coming down for a free weekend.'

Rotarian Jim Franks, head of the local convalescent home for sick children, who doubled up in the summer as a Punch and Judy man on the beach, chimed in. 'Why not make it a family competition', he said, 'with the kids of the winning entry being the ones to press the button? It would be just their scene. Fancy going back to school on Monday and being able to say you spent the weekend setting off an explosion to blow up a pier. Terrific.' He laughed adding, 'I bet nobody would believe you!' Jim called most of the ideas that came to him terrific. Mostly, they weren't. But this one was acknowledged as such by his fellow Rotarians.

So it was that, in due course, a national competition was arranged, the prize for the winner being an all-expenses paid family weekend at Spraycombe. During the stay, the children in the family would take part in a spectacular public event in which they would blow the legs off the pier so that its superstructure sank into the shallows, ready to be taken apart.

The Firth family lived in Birmingham. There was father, mother and two daughters, Lucy and Julie, who were eleven and thirteen. Seeing a free weekend in Spraycombe advertised on a poster at Birmingham New Street station when he was returning from a business trip, father mentioned it at home. 'Remember when we went to Spraycombe when you girls were small? How would you like to go there again for a weekend?' Julie screwed up her nose: 'Dad, we're too big for building sandcastles.' Lucy backed her sister: 'Isn't that the grotty place where we couldn't go on the pier because it was falling down?' Alex Firth explained. 'The collapsing pier is the whole point. There's a competition about it.' The girls had been keen on competitions ever since Julie won two tickets to a Boyzone concert by being first out of the hat with the names of each member of the group. Their father delivered them to the venue and sat for three hours outside to bring his daughters home afterwards. When he moaned to his wife about it she said, 'It's called parenthood, Alex.'

It was agreed that mother would write to obtain details of the Spraycombe competition. 'Anybody could answer these questions', announced Lucy when the entry form arrived. 'Of course', said Jane Firth, 'hundreds of families will send in the right answers. It's like the Boyzone thing – the luck of the draw.' 'Well, that rules us out,' said her husband, 'I've never won anything in all my life.' 'But darling', responded his wife, with just a hint of irony in her voice, 'you won me!' The girls looked at one another and raised their eyes to heaven. Later Lucy observed to her sister how embarrassing it was when parents got romantic. She thought old people should be past that sort of thing.

A huge crowd lined the Spraycombe seafront to watch Lucy and Julie Firth, who had come all the way from Birmingham with their proud parents to blow up the derelict remains of the old pier. Councillors had expressed satisfaction to one another over the fact that the privilege had fallen to a family from Birmingham. That was, they knew, a place where crime and disorder were rampant. It was not, of course, a city any of them had ever visited but, as Councillor Brigden had said, all big cities were the same and in Birmingham, as he understood it, the people had not yet reached the stage of development where they spoke the Queen's English. 'There was a local government spokesman from Birmingham on television', said Councillor Hunstanton, 'who pronounced his vowels in a most peculiar manner. Goodness know what he might do with a diphthong.' Cyril Hunstanton, OBE, who had retired to Spraycombe after a civil service career, was very particular about the proper use of English. In the present case, the other councillors were sure he knew what he was talking about, despite being unaware themselves of the difference between a diphthong and a dishwasher. All in all, they felt, Spraycombe had every right to bask in the glory of having brought relief to a family from one of England's third-world-type territories.

There was a moment of tension as Florrie Simpson held up the bright yellow flag to signal that the explosion was imminent. When it fell, the two girls, each with a finger on the button set in place by the demolition men, pressed down hard. The superstructure standing in the water rose in the air, with smoke and spray billowing beneath its rusty frame, then sank quite gracefully into the sea. Only the upper part of the bandstand could be seen after the smoke cleared. Councillor Choke raised her handkerchief to one eye to catch a droplet that glistened on an eyelash. 'How sad', she muttered, 'how very sad.' Next day, the story of the blowing up of Spraycombe pier was widely reported. There was even an account in The Times, which the director of leisure services copied to all councillors, with a note to say that the town had never before had so much as a mention in the quality press. He also reported that the entry fees for the competition, at £5 a time, had brought in a considerable sum. The exact figure would be presented at the next council meeting, but it would more than pay the account of the demolition company and might also, perhaps, pay for redecoration of the council chamber. Councillors had been talking about it for three years. George Brigden was of the view that the dilapidated state of the chamber diminished what he called 'the dignity and authority of the council'.

Spraycombe's moment of fame soon passed, but it gave an enormous boost to the town's morale, not to mention the councillors' opinion of themselves.

George Brigden was able, without much difficulty, to persuade himself that he had been in favour of Henry Butler's proposal from the start. Any reservations he expressed were simply exploratory. Agnes Choke, after a period of mourning, came to terms with her bereavement and settled for relating to anyone who would listen stories of when, on the dear old pier, she was Spaycombe's dancing queen.

Lucy Firth had always enjoyed reading and writing in primary school. In her first year at secondary she had quickly distinguished herself in English lessons. Her teacher, Miss Bennett, nicknamed Lizzie by those she taught, sang her praises in the staffroom and persuaded the head of English to include one of her poems in the school magazine. But today, she was aghast. 'This cannot be', she said to herself, as she marked Lucy's work. 'What can't?', inquired a colleague sitting nearby. 'It's Lucy Firth', came the reply, 'I told them to write about how they spent last weekend and she's come up with some ridiculous tale about going to the seaside and blowing up a pier.' 'I thought Lucy was one of your star pupils', replied the colleague, 'what can have got into her?' One of the PE staff thought she knew. 'It's the hormones. They have the funniest effect on some girls. But it's a bit early for one of Lucy's age to be seriously affected.'

Grace Luker, head of history, who had been at the school for as long as anyone could remember, and who seemed to be part of the history she taught, raised her head from Walter Bagehot's book on the English constitution. He it was who wrote that school teachers should have an atmosphere of awe, and walk wonderingly, as if amazed at being themselves. It was a message that Grace seemed to have taken to heart. Her progress along the school's corridors had a degree of stateliness that left some new young teachers open-mouthed on first observing it. Unsurprisingly, the head of history was known by girls and teachers as Amazing Grace. Responding to Miss Bennett's concern, she declared: 'You surprise me. You obviously don't read *The Times*.' She paused to allow the awfulness of such a discovery to sink in then went on, 'The Firths did indeed go to some obscure seaside resort and blow up its pier last weekend. They won a competition to do it.' She paused for thought. 'You know', she said, 'we have never had anyone from this school do something so unusual. The head ought to report it in her speech at prizegiving.'

And so it came to pass that what happened one day, at a small and unnoticed seaside town, was proclaimed at an annual school gathering in a mighty city far from the sea. People still go to Spraycombe to see the spot where the event occurred. The remains of the pier have long been removed. All there is to see where it once stood is the relentless movement of the tide in and out, in and out. But the councillors of Spraycombe have put up a plaque on the promenade nearby, as a result of a proposal by Agnes Choke, seconded by George Brigden, to mark the spot where history was made during a weekend break.

# A KIND OF CONTENTMENT

'I told you, didn't I? I told you what it would be like! The man is drunk with power and a complete fool. He struts around in that gown thinking he's God's gift to the education system.' Jack Stanley's furious verdict on the new headmaster could be heard throughout the staff room, in which he and his colleagues in the English department occupied their usual chairs in one corner.

Jack's outburst had been prompted by the appearance on the staff room notice board of an announcement that James Burt of the sixth form would not be entered for one of his A level subjects, namely economics. His persistent idleness had, said the notice, convinced the head of economics that he had no chance of passing so the cost to the local authority of entering him was not justified.

'You know what this means, don't you?', said Jack to those around him, 'It means his university application will be a waste of time. No decent place will make an offer to someone taking only two A levels.' The speaker stood up and shouted down the room, 'It's all because you economists haven't been able to motivate one of the brightest lads in this school.'

Nearby, Susan Jacques, in her first year of teaching French, looked in wonder at the giant of a man, his unkempt beard shaking with fury, who made this proclamation. She thought: 'I bet he terrifies them in the classroom. Wish I could. They terrify me.' Matt Draper, 28, history, looked in wonder at the very attractive young woman having these thoughts. With a staff numbering over a hundred, he had not noticed her before. He thought: 'I must get to know her.'

Glynis Havelock, 58, who ran the catering course in the middle and upper school that had enabled several of those choosing it to find careers in the kitchens of London hotels, was unimpressed by Jack Stanley. She had seen similar histrionics over the years and the perpetrators rarely came to much in the teaching profession. They became frustrated and ended up working in teacher training institutions, advancing radical solutions to the perceived ills of the education system. With a bit of luck, their ideas were published and received the serious attention of politicians searching for new, headline-grabbing answers to the persistent problems of school discipline and how to improve examination results. Glynis remembered with scorn the years when mixed ability teaching was popular among teacher trainers and inspectors.

Glynis approved of the new headmaster, who showed signs of putting the clock back to the good old days. She thought his wearing a gown gave a certain academic status to the school, especially at prizegiving. She also liked the way he referred to those staying on after sixteen as sixth formers. She regarded the modern jargon with distaste. Fancy talking about post-sixteen students. Were none of the old traditions to be preserved?

Darren Baker (15) hated the school. He reckoned he had learned nothing in his years there. He hated most of the other pupils too, especially those who always had their exercise books and handed in their homework. Teachers no longer expected Darren to co-operate. Most just ignored him if he turned up, asking nothing of him in the hope that he wouldn't cause trouble. He often skipped lessons for a smoke in the toilets, or went up to the amusement arcade in the town. His truancy was never properly investigated as those who were supposed to teach him preferred it if he was absent. It meant they could actually focus on those who wanted to learn. He had been the subject of a supervision order after persistently thieving from local shops, but not much supervision had taken place. The social worker responsible for seeing him, a girl not many years older than Darren, was frightened of him. John Stockford (head of year 5) believed, and often stated, that quite a few social workers were fearful of the responsibilities laid upon them. He argued that child abuse in the home often went unchecked because social workers were apprehensive about challenging violent parents.

Darren's anger at the school, which was part of his discontentment with the rest of his life, had recently been exacerbated by what the new headmaster, whom he referred to as the cock of this here dung heap – a title he had picked up from a Jimmy Cagney gangster film - confiscated his heavy boots. He knew they weren't allowed, but they were part of his armoury against the world. He used them to smash the bottom panels in the school's swing doors when he was angry, and to kick those who got in his way when the corridors were crowded. Walking about in the trainers he had been given to wear instead had people laughing at him, which fed his fury. He resolved to get his own back. He thought a lot about what he might do to show that he was a person it was unsafe to cross.

John Stears (geography), who dreaded the arrival of Darren in his lessons, dropped into a chair in the staff room after a particularly bad run-in with the boy. His face was red with fury. He was in his second year of teaching and was, in the opinion of some of his colleagues, in the wrong job. The disorder in his lessons was infectious. Anyone teaching a class right after it had been with John Stears had to spend the first few minutes quietening everybody down. He said: 'That Darren Baker is a head case. He told me he would like to torch this place. I wish to God someone would set fire to *him*. I'd like to watch the bugger burn.'

The huge school, had been created in spectacular new buildings by amalgamating three rival institutions – a grammar school and two secondary moderns. The disastrous consequences had been predicted by all but the politicians and bureaucrats at county hall. In the early years, previous rivals set out to knock hell out of one another. Things had settled down since, but people in the local community still talked about the school's first difficulties, which included knife fights in the playgrounds and attacks on teachers. Those with no appetite for education had enjoyed discovering ways of preventing it taking place. Pitching desks and chairs out of windows several floors up was a particular favourite.

Someone who had no problems with discipline was Jack Stanley. He was proud of his reputation for being able to break up a playground fight at fifty paces. His advance on a crowd watching such a spectacle caused it to melt away and those fighting suddenly to discover that they were best mates and just mucking about.

Jack, who challenged authority in all its forms, would allow no questioning of his own. Woe betide any pupil who misbehaved when he was teaching. Towering over a miscreant, shaking with fury, he would boomingly declare: 'I've never seen anything like it in all me life!' Pausing for effect, he would then announce what awaited any further misbehaviour in a quietly sinister voice: 'If you want trouble, my name's trouble.' From time to time, at staff meetings, Jack would explain the secret of classroom control. 'Teaching', he would say, 'is a form of acting. The classroom is simply a theatre in which we perform.' But John Stears had been heard to respond by observing that it was fine for someone of the size and acting ability of Jack Stanley to say such things, but that wasn't what he had been taught by his PGCE lecturers. Philip Raeburn, head of sixth form, believed that Jack's charisma was the result of his total commitment to building a new world order. A member of the Socialist Workers Party, he looked for the overthrow of capitalism and its self-serving agents of tyranny, among whom he counted head teachers.

Graham Tuck, headmaster, had been in post just long enough to have discovered who among the staff were for him and who against. Jack Stanley, for all his bluster, did not worry him; quite the opposite. He was a first-rate classroom teacher and his political opinions were treated with amused contempt by most of his colleagues. 'When the revolution comes', observed Lionel Westbury, head of economics, 'Jack will want to be in charge, and God help anyone who refuses to man the barricades. He will make the Terror during the French Revolution seem like a picnic.'

James Burt (sixth form) was in the mood for revolution. Okay, he had been warned about not getting down to work in economics several times, and his last three essays had each been graded EUU. It had been hoped that the E would wake him up to the need to take the subject seriously but it had had the opposite effect. Seeing the E, he had thought, 'Well, that's a pass of sorts. I'll be alright as long as I don't get down to unclassified.' When his next effort was graded U, he felt sure he was being deliberately messed about. He knew he could pass at A level by using his wits. His father was a local councillor and a member of the school's governing body and it had never occurred to James that the new head would refuse to enter him for economics. What a cheek! He would get his dad to come up and sort out the stupid man.

Lionel Westbury was surprised when the head had first asked him if the boy in question deserved to be entered. The answer he gave was a simple, 'No.' Lionel had explained that James Burt was bone idle and conceitedly convinced that he could handle the A level economics examination on the strength of his innate outstanding ability. The marks he had been given for his essays seemed not to bother him.

The boy appeared to believe that, when the time came, he would do a spot of swotting and surprise everyone. As for the suggestion that the money spent by the local education authority on entering him would be wasted, he smiled knowingly, secure in the conviction that his natural intelligence would see him through.

Graham Tuck's decision delighted the head of economics, although he had not expected to be supported. He had not experienced such decisiveness before. 'Will cutting Burt out not mean trouble?', he asked. 'Undoubtedly', came the reply, 'but it will be my job to deal with that.'

In the event, Mr Burt's rage knew no bounds, especially when he discovered that only the place where he had been taught could enter his son for his examinations. Even Jack Stanley was impressed with the way Graham Tuck had stood up to the abominable Mr Burt, who had a reputation for throwing his weight about. 'I could change my mind about this man', said Jack, 'he's ready to stick up for the workers.'

Darren Baker would have been surprised to know that anyone choosing to stay on at school intending to go to university could become a problem. He thought it was only people like him who got into trouble. Still seething over the confiscation of his boots, he settled on starting a fire at the school pavilion when no one was about, watching it go up with great satisfaction. It was an ancient wooden structure that had stood in the field long before the school was built. In an advanced state of disrepair, the PE staff were not sorry to see it go. Might a new pavilion rise from the ashes?

Darren's act of arson did not, as he had hoped, go unobserved. A neighbour whose back garden overlooked the school field had seen what he did. Mrs Binks seemed to know everything that went on in the community. She bustled in to the local police station the morning after the fire to give her report to the inspector, who had met her many times before. 'It was that boy Baker done that fire at the school', she announced, 'I know 'is tricks. Bin over my fence stealin' more than once. A right toe rag. But I feel sorry for 'im. Can't even start a fire without bein' caught. Not even any good as a juveenile delickwant.'

Nobody on the school staff who had ever attempted to teach Darren was surprised about what he had done. 'As thick as a post and nasty with it', said Laura Tate, head of maths, 'I can't imagine what his parents make of him.' Jenny Laker, who worked in the remedial department, helping slow learners, was incensed. Normally disinclined to join in staff room gossip, she said: 'That's no way to talk about someone whose education is in our hands. Most of his life Darren's been fostered. He has never lasted long with any foster parents. No wonder he has never found any kind of security and contentment.' It was unlike Jenny to unload her feelings in the staff room. Several of her hearers didn't know who she was.

Jenny's little speech re-launched the regular staff room debate about the school's responsibilities towards its students. 'Baker is not the sort to get anything out of being at school. He needs a different sort of place.' Thus spoke Charles Dean, a tall, imposing man who regarded himself as a fount of wisdom as head of religious education. He had been an RE teacher for ten years following about the same amount of time as an Anglican parish priest, in which role he had upset his church wardens. One of the staff room comedians piped up, 'A different sort of place for the likes of Darren Baker? You mean with the gorillas in a zoo?', said Ted Winter, who taught geography now that he was too old to continue as a PE specialist. Ted's philosophy of education was unsophisticated. His words on entering a class room were always the same: 'Now, you lot, sit down and shut up. That's *all* you have to do for the next forty minutes.'

Some who had taught in the grammar school that had been joined with the two secondary moderns to create the comprehensive school when it opened continued to believe that success in public examinations was the purpose of education. Young people lacking academic ability ought not, they believed, to be allowed to trouble the system. Such teachers were prepared to admit that they had no idea what should be done with them. 'Governments have struggled for years in search of an answer to that problem', insisted Roger Gaunt, head of physics. The one thing he was sure of was they should not be inflicted on his department.

Graham Tuck was sorry Mrs Binks had gone to the police about the pavilion. He had some sympathy for Darren Baker in view of his background and had hoped he would see his time out at school and slip away quietly into the world beyond. He thought: 'Pity about his boots.' He decided to have a staff meeting. As the great army of teachers gathered, over one hundred in number, including part-timers, there was an expectant buzz. The James Burt and Darren Baker incidents had caused a stir.

The headmaster identified two questions as being fundamental to the school's future development. What should be done to ensure that the students were stretched? What should be done to meet the needs of those without academic ability? 'This', declared Graham Tuck, 'is a comprehensive school. Those we are working with are not all equally clever, but every single one is equally valuable.'

Jack Stanley thought, 'My God, he's one of us. He cares about the proletariat.' Glynis Havelock thought, 'What he's saying doesn't have anything to do with the catering course.' Laura Tate thought, 'So what's to be done about the shortage of maths teachers? Kids like Baker have nothing but supply teachers most of the time. No wonder they're turned off.' Charles Dean thought, 'I'm down to take assembly tomorrow and I'm out tonight. I'll have to do it off the cuff. They never listen anyway.' Susan Jacques thought, 'How can I teach French to those who can't read English properly?' Matt Draper thought, looking across at Susan, 'I really must get to know her.' Graham Tuck thought, looking at what he saw as an amazing gathering of teachers, 'How on earth can they be encouraged to work as a team? They have such different approaches to teaching.'

Discussion continued for about an hour, then Graham made his way back to his study. A giant of a man was waiting to see him. He looked very aggressive. 'Good afternoon' said Graham, 'can I help you?' The man grabbed the headmaster's shoulder. 'You lot got my Darren in trouble with the filth. Damn the lot of you.' He smashed his fist into the headmaster's face, breaking his nose.

Despite pressure from county hall, Graham declined to bring charges against his assailant. He thought a broken nose was no big deal. He had experienced it twice before, once in his younger days, when playing rugby for Saracens third fifteen, and once when one of his own boys had jumped on him during a rather over-exuberant beach game. But, although he would have preferred to deal with what had occurred in his own way, the bright and shining ones at county hall insisted on holding an inquiry. Cecily Briggs, an elected member of the local education authority who regarded herself as having a considerable understanding of what she called pedagogical issues, having lectured on the philosophy of education at one of the newer universities, gave her verdict on what had occurred: 'It is very important for schools to establish good relations with parents. There was obviously a breakdown in this case. If the boy was unhappy in school, were his parents not invited to school for a discussion? It must review its arrangements for parental involvement.'

The school's district inspector, who knew its problems well, and the homes from which some of its most difficult pupils came, interjected: 'Some parents don't want to be involved, you know. They wouldn't even bother to look at a letter of invitation, even if they were capable of reading it.' 'What a cynical attitude', said Cecily Briggs, taking umbrage, 'I'm surprised that the inspectorate think like that.' 'I'm not being cynical', said Brian Kelly, 'some parents had a bad experience of school themselves and don't want to know about their children's failures and misdemeanours. What's more, some parents are members of the criminal fraternity.'

He paused, then added for effect: 'As in the case we are discussing.' 'Good heavens, you don't say!', declared Sir Gerald Price, an aged party worthy who had difficulty in following proceedings at meetings. In the end, it was decided that the county education officer should write to all head teachers, encouraging them to establish close relations with parents, notwithstanding the difficulty of doing so in some cases, of which the education authority was fully aware.

While all this was going on, the young man who had provoked the discussion had made a life-defining choice. He had taken to the streets round London's Charing Cross. To his surprise, he found himself readily accepted by the cardboard community, so called because many slept in cardboard boxes. Its members quickly educated him in matters like where to wait for the soup run, where the best pitches were for handouts and how to stake a claim for a corner in which to sleep. He was surprised at the way in which his new friends were ready to share such important information. One of them, a shabby man with a plummy voice explained: 'It's the camaraderie of affliction, old chap. We're all escaping from something horrid.'

Although Darren's schooling had not equipped him for this way of life, he took to it without difficulty. Wrapped in a blanket provided by the Sally Ann, settling in the corner of a shop doorway, a paper cup of hot soup in his hand, he looked at the stars overhead and told himself, 'I'm free. Free at last. Like that bloke said in America.' So Darren Baker acquired a kind of contentment.

# EVENTS

'Life', said Sir Alan Fordbridge, 'is not lived as to time but as to events. One can coast along for years with nothing unexpected happening. Then one memorable event can alter the whole direction of one's life.'

Alan's family had heard the pronouncement many times. 'Father', said his youngest daughter, 'please don't go all philosophical when Simon comes.' The other members of the family murmured agreement, Jane, the eldest, most vehemently.

There were three daughters, all born within a year of one another. Jane and Sarah were in their first and second years at Cambridge, one reading history and the other languages. Rebellious Poppy, the youngest, was heading for the LSE. Her determination to ignore Oxbridge had shocked the head of the ancient grammar school where the three girls had distinguished academic records. 'But what will your parents say?', asked the head-mistress, Miss Horbridge, with astonishment, peering over her glasses. Poppy, whom some of the staff referred to as a rather challenging member of the upper sixth, thought: 'It's not their lives, it's mine!'

Jane had got to know Simon at Corpus. His imminent visit to Jane's home made both of them nervous. 'Is this so the family patriarch can give me the once-over as a suitable person to know?' he asked. 'Of course', came the laughing reply, 'we are a very patriarchal family. What father says, goes.' Her laughter subsided and she added, 'At least, that's what we like him to think. It keeps him happy.'

'You mean, you fake submission?' responded Simon, propped up on one elbow in bed, looking down at Sarah. She said, 'It avoids trouble with people of dad's generation. But don't imagine it will carry over into ours. No way, boyo.' Simon laughed. 'No, I can't imagine you being submissive', he said. 'Wait till you meet my sister Poppy', warned Jane, 'she's for the revolution next Tuesday at the latest.' Simon said, 'I'm looking forward to meeting her. Is she as beautiful as you?' Jane punched him in the chest. 'Never you mind about that', she said, 'just you keep your mind on me.' 'Not just my mind', came the response as he took Jane in his arms.

As the couple drove down to Camberley, Jane was in buoyant mood. 'Just think', she said, 'before long, Cambridge will be behind us. Are you really going to take that job in the Matrix Chambers? It'll be a good start but it will be years before you make the legal big time.' They had had this discussion before. ‘You know I don’t aim for what you call the legal big time. I hope to get a safe seat in parliament within five years.’

‘Well, young man’, said Sir Alan Forbridge, senior consultant in neurology at Great Ormond Street Hospital, ‘what does your future hold?’ Sitting round the dinner table with the rest of the family, Jane exchanged glances with Simon and thought, ‘Oh dear. Here we go. Dad wants to know Simon’s prospects.’

‘I should warn you, Simon,’ said Sir Alan, ‘that my daughters are a great disappointment to me. None of them is interested in studying medicine.’ ‘That’s easy to explain’, interjected Poppy, a small, bouncy girl with rosy cheeks and a ready smile who looked younger than her eighteen years. Jane fixed her eyes pleadingly on her, as if to say, ‘Please, please don’t say what I know you are going to say.’ Poppy said, ‘The medical profession is in the grip of dominant males. Father, you have brought us up to be self-confident, so don’t be surprised that some of us want to change the world. But we won’t start with the medical profession. It’s the most powerful bastion of male dominance of all.’

Sarah, exquisitely beautiful, the quiet one, was not listening to the exchanges. Her mind was elsewhere. She was wondering how to tell the family what was on her mind. She had been thinking about that for several days. With a visitor present, she realized she had an excuse to put it off a little longer. But Andre was pressing her to make it known that she was dropping out and going with him when he returned to France. She knew what the reaction would be. Only Poppy would admire her striking out; her determination to escape from the suffocation of Cambridge and Camberley.

Sarah felt that she had arrived at her decision without thinking too much about it. Life in Camberley had followed a pattern undetermined by her. There had never been any question that she would move from the local primary school to the grammar school and then to university, almost certainly to Oxford or Cambridge. Miss Horbridge recommended Cambridge because she believed one met a rather better class of student there. She did not want her girls to be mixing with the Balliol rabble, as she put it. 'Too many reds', she claimed. It was going to take her a long time to recover from Poppy Forbridge's choice of LSE.

Sarah continued to think about how to tell her parents that she was in love with her French tutor and was about to go with him to Paris. 'Sarah, what do you think?', asked her mother. 'About what?', came the reply. Lady Forbridge sighed resignedly. 'About Monet's garden that we went to see when you were studying the Impressionists at school and we wanted to make sure you were up to speed on them. We wanted you to be able to say you had been there.' Seeing that her daughters were up to speed had been her most determined occupation as they grew up.

Sheila Forbridge was a formidable woman. Bossy, according to their friends in talking about her to one another. Committed to organizing the lives of others according to what she knew was best for them. Her version of how people should lead their lives was not always appreciated, but she was not deterred. Serving others could be a hurtful activity, as Jesus had shown. Lady Forbridge's understanding of the Bible was quite basic. She had no truck with what she called the God-is-no-more brigade. Just as Jesus was out to save the world, so she was out to save the people in her bit of it, whether or not they wanted it.

Simon responded to what Poppy had said about dominant males. He said, 'The House of Commons is pretty full of male chauvinists. It filled up a bit with squeaky females when Blair's babes arrived, but they've yet to make a great difference to the atmosphere. But things are changing, and I'm glad of that, because I aim to be there a few years from now.' Sir Alan's eyebrows rose. 'So', he said, 'you're interested in politics. I thought you were reading law. Jane gave us the idea that you were going to be a wealthy barrister one day, then onward and upward to the bench.'

'Dear Lord', prayed Jane, 'don't let Simon get

going about politics.' But the prayer was too late. 'To tell the truth', said Simon, 'I'm more interested in making the law than applying it. That's the only way to make a real difference to the state of things in this class-ridden society.' Lady Forbridge was appalled. Poppy was ecstatic. Here was her kind of man. She smiled delightedly across the table at Jane. 'The trouble is', continued Simon, 'the best laid political plans face one enormous problem. When he was prime minister, Harold Macmillan was asked what made government so difficult. He replied: 'Events, dear boy, events.' Mind you, that's not just a political phenomenon. The best laid plans of mice and men go astray. Steinbeck has written a brilliant novel about that.'

Poppy could not restrain herself. 'Simon, you're at the wrong university. You ought to be at the LSE. That's where the big thinking is being done to remake the world. Class-ridden is right. Just look at us round this table. Poverty and deprivation are outside our experience. People like us don't really want to know about those at the bottom of the pile.' 'Now just you hold on, Poppy', said her father. 'There are no class distinctions in my operating theatre. Many of the families I deal with, who come to my clinic desperate about their sick children, are at the bottom of the pile, as you put it. We receive all comers.'

Sheila Forbridge decided it was time to speak up

for her husband. She addressed Poppy forcefully. 'Your father doesn't take private patients, as you well know. Some of his colleagues think he's a fool but he is as committed as anybody on this planet to using his skills to serve all sorts and conditions of men.' Hullo, thought Simon, Jane's mother is into the Book of Common Prayer. Without thinking – a weakness Jane had warned him about several times – he said out loud what was in his mind: 'O God, the creator and preserver of all mankind, we humbly beseech thee for all sorts and conditions of men; that thou wouldest be pleased to make thy ways known unto them, thy saving health unto all nations.' Lady Forbridge stopped being appalled. She found herself thinking that Simon was redeemable from some of his more extravagant political opinions. She said, 'Now isn't that a beautiful prayer? How can those happy clappy people think they have a better way of addressing God?'

As dinner proceeded, the conversation wandered to and fro, touching a variety of subjects. It had no particular direction but served to reveal those round the table to one another, sometimes deliberately, sometimes unintentionally.

It was dark and raining when Simon and Jane prepared to set off back to Cambridge. Sarah hitched a lift from them, having come down by train for the occasion. As they proceeded northwards, with the wipers beating a tattoo on the windscreen, Simon said, 'How come that your parents have produced a radical daughter like Poppy? But I suppose that, with three daughters, it was always likely that one wouldn't conform.'

'Be not deceived', said Sarah. 'none of us lives the way they think we do. You two are sleeping together, aren't you? And as for me ...', she paused, wondering whether to tell her secret. 'As for me', she said, 'I'm dropping out and going to France with Andre at the end of term.' Jane gasped. 'Oh Sarah, are you sure you know what you're doing?' Sarah's response left no room for doubt. 'Andre is the goods. He's wonderful. I'm in love with him. Life without him when he returns home would be ...', she paused, as was her habit when moved to emotion, '... no life at all. There would be no more sun.' She recalled some lines learned when she was studying Milton's 'Samson Agonistes'. 'Dark, dark, dark amid the blaze of noon, irrecoverably dark, without all hope of day'. That's how it would be without Andre.

Simon said, 'Good for you, Sarah. Grasp the moment, that's what I say. Never mind what your parents think. They'll come round. Mine did when my sister went off with an aeronautical engineer. Sophie warned me she was about to take flight with an aero boffin before she told mum and dad. There was a bit of a scene but now we're all happy again. Time's a great healer.' Sarah was not so sure. 'Time heals as long as events don't intervene', she said, unaware of how prophetic were her words. Jane said, 'Life is not lived as to time but as to events.' 'That's profound', responded Simon. 'It's father's favourite aphorism,' came the reply.

Ten minutes later, the car smashed head on into a jeep coming round a bend on the wrong side of the road. The night was dark and wet. Four other vehicles drove into the smash-up. The bodies of Simon and his passengers had to be cut from the wreckage. Only Sarah survived, with half her brain caved in. She never went to France with Andre. Poppy never went to the LSE. She stayed at home to help her broken mother cope with Sarah, who needed twenty-four hour support. Sir Alan Forbridge added private patients to his NHS list. Some said he preferred to be at the hospital to being at home. When his brother, a GP, asked him one day how his family was coping, he replied, half-mocking his well-known personal philosophy, 'Not very well. We've been defeated by events, dear boy, defeated by events.'

# FORGIVENESS

The seething crowd at St Pancras reflected James Lister's state of mind. He knew his business trip to Brussels was futile. Why was he going? Because he needed an opportunity, away from home, to end his troubles. One possibility had already taken hold of him.

A tall, athletic man in his forties, his expensive suit and confident stride suggested a man accustomed to success. Clutching his briefcase and overnight bag, he headed for the underground and descended on the escalator towards the platform that would take him to Heathrow. He was conscious of a mass of people around him, living normal lives, who would in due course return to domestic security at the end of the day. No such prospect lay ahead for Lister. He was a ruined man and would take his family with him down into the dark valley of penury.

He had read about men who put an end to their worries by throwing themselves under the wheels of an underground train. It would surely not be all that hard to bring himself to do it.

His pace slowed as the awesome moment of decision approached. Just twenty yards more, and he would be on the platform. His stomach contracted as he realized how little time he had left. He stopped to gather himself and his gaze wandered to a poster on the wall. It was an Art on the Underground reproduction. He stood transfixed before Edvard Munch's most stunning work: *The Scream*.

Munch had painted the original in Berlin in 1893. When first displayed, it had given people nightmares. A typical work of the Expressionist school, it depicted man's inner turmoil. Munch once said: 'Just as Leonardo da Vinci dissected the human anatomy, so I dissect man's soul.' Here was a human face, alone in a grey landscape, the mouth stretched wide in terror and despair.

Lister stood rooted to the spot as people jostled past him. In the tortured face in the picture he saw something of his own condition. But, even more powerfully, he saw his wife's reaction to what he had in mind. He could hear her saying, 'Why? Why? We could manage on nothing. We did before.' He moved away and joined the crowd on the platform, then boarded the train that would take him to the airport. He would catch his flight to Brussels and decide what to do later. He had become very good at putting off difficult decisions.

On landing in Brussels, he made his way to the train that would take him to the city centre and found himself a seat in a quiet corner of a carriage. Arriving at the Gare Central, he crossed the station concourse, buying a waffle at the stall there. He was comforted by this simple customary act as he headed for his hotel on the Rue Duquesnoy.

As he passed through the Grand Place, with its spectacular baroque buildings, he lifted his eyes to the top of the magnificent tower on the old town hall. The gigantic golden weather cock was swinging to and fro, buffeted by a high wind. James Lister thought: 'Me too.'

He felt uneasy booking in at the Royal Windsor. He had always done so before, then as now, at the firm's expense, but it seemed outrageous to do so today. Then he thought: 'To hell with it. Why not live it up before I go.'

He could not face doing business in Brussels on what was going to be the last day of his life. He rang the firm's office near the Bourse and explained that he would not be coming. Then he set off to walk round the city for while and make up his mind what to do. As usual, this footsteps took him to St Michael's Cathedral.

Lister stood before the most dramatic and awesome pulpit in Christendom, rising twenty feet or more towards the cathedral's roof. Built of wood that glowed red against its flanking stone pillars, it depicted the Fall of Man. Winding round it, from base to summit, was the figure of a serpent. Adam and Eve cowered at the base, the woman clutching the forbidden fruit. Peering round the pulpit's side at the unfortunate pair was a skeleton. Lister had always admired the beauty of the craftsmanship, but today the imagery of a man's surrender to temptation seared his soul.

Shaken, he rushed from the cathedral and crossed the road to the sanctuary of a favourite coffee shop in the Rue Ravenstein. He gloomily sat and asked himself again what on earth he should do. He stirred his drink and the foam on the surface went round and round, like his thoughts.

Speculating had been hugely profitable for a few years. He had showered his wife with gifts, explaining his wealth as the outcome of bonuses earned for his performance as sales manager of Eurocom, a firm manufacturing telecommunications equipment for the European market. When the big bonus days were over, James was still able to encourage Carol in the belief that business was booming: the media were constantly talking about the telecommunications explosion. But in fact competition was becoming fiercer all the time and Eurocom's leading place in the market had been surrendered some time ago. New men with new ideas were taking over. On top of that, regulation of the industry was growing and changing the commercial landscape in which the industry operated.

Lister had gambled on the stock market because

the bonuses were no longer rolling in. The crunch came when his speculative activity backfired. With a sinking heart, he discovered that his grasp of which way things were heading was not as reliable as he thought. His shares fell dramatically, and at such a speed that he could not unload them to retrieve the situation. Now the house would have to go, and the BMW, and the expensive lifestyle to which he and his wife had grown accustomed. They would be reduced to penury. James wondered how they would find the money to eat, his mind having passed beyond rational thought.

James felt physically sick as a result of what was going on in his head. Most agonizing of all was the prospect of having to confess to his wife what he had done. It was impossible. He wouldn't be able to look her in the eye. He bowed his head over his cold coffee and wept, his posture not unlike that of Adam in the cathedral carving.

He left the coffee shop and headed up the Rue Ravenstein towards the art museum at the Place Royale. On previous visits to this, one of his favourite places in Brussels, where he had often whiled away and hour or two between business appointments, he had sought out the Monets and the Reniors. He moved through the concourse inside the entrance with that in mind. Then, for the second time that day, he stopped in his tracks and stood rooted to the spot.

The sculpture must have been there before, but he had not noticed it. Now it confronted him like a message from God. Pierre Braecke's masterpiece in marble, carved in 1893, the year in which Edvard Munch produced *The Scream*, reached into his heart and mind. A man is on his knees before a woman, his head turned slightly upward. One of the woman's arms clutches him to her; a hand supports his head as she bends to kiss him.

The two figures, though carved from stone, seemed to Lister to breathe, the man with panting desperation, the woman softly, with quiet delight. There was no condemnation in the woman's posture, only gratitude for the man's return. The sculpture's title was *Le Pardon*. Forgiveness. Lister sat cross-legged on the floor and stared at the sculpture for a long time. Then he got to his feet and headed home.

As far as is known, Edvard Munch never met Pierre Braecke, although they were contemporaries. They were never to know that they had each created a work of art in the year 1893 that would, viewed one day a century or more later, save a man's life.

# AN EASTER STORY

The number of pipes on the church organ was the same as the last time he had counted, a few minutes ago. Tom Didsbury switched his attention back to the sermon. The preacher was talking about Mary Magdalene at the garden tomb on the first Easter morning.

> *Here we have in John's wonderful Gospel one of the most moving passages in all scripture. What a scenario! A garden in springtime; an empty tomb; a missing body; a desolate woman; angels; a mysterious figure moving among the blossoming trees; a moment of recognition and discovery; a reunion of stunning power; a message of hope for the future.*

Tom thought of Mary, his wife at home. She had raged at him, on and off, for most of Saturday after the mail was delivered. 'Tom Didsbury', she had raged, 'What on earth did you think you were doing? Have you given up on our marriage? I want you out of here by Monday.' He had tried to calm her down but his one-night stand with Lucy, his young practice nurse, looked disastrous.

> *We have special ways of talking to those closest to us, don't we? My wife only uses my full name when she's really exasperated. Normally, I'm just Jim, but when I'm making a mess of something, she says, 'James Reynolds, what on earth are you doing?' When I want to get round her I call her my little tumbling waterfall of affection. It used to work better than it does now. After twenty years of marriage, she is wise to my stratagems.*

Mrs Evans, church steward, thought to herself that living with the Reverend James Reynolds must be a real challenge. Such a disorganized minister she had never come across before, and one who freely admitted his uselessness at home. He had once made known from the pulpit that changing a light bulb was for him a major engineering exercise. He explained this after a local paper reported that the bishop of the diocese had been hospitalized after attempting to change a light bulb by climbing on a chair placed on a table. His episcopal eminence fractured his pelvis when he fell off.*

Tom Didsbury's thoughts followed a different

* An actual event when the Right Reverend Peter Dawes was Bishop of Derby, widely reported at the time, which caused a good deal of good-natured banter by his cathedral colleagues.

pattern from those of Mrs Evans after hearing the preacher's words. It was almost as if he was aware of Tom's situation. No way, he concluded, and gave his attention to two young people sitting in front of him. He could tell they were holding hands. They had grown up in the church, fell in love, and planned to marry soon. Tom recalled his falling in love with Mary. But what now? How was he to face the situation he had created?

> *You know, the Lord we come here to worship knows about the situations we face. We all have things we are ashamed of; things we wouldn't want those around us in church this morning to know about; things you wouldn't want me to know about. Let me impress you with a bit of Latin: sunt lacrimae rerum. Virgil wrote that thousands of years ago. It means: there are tears in life. Suffering cannot be avoided. Jesus knew all about that. He has been there. Today we celebrate his resurrection, but there would have been no such event if there had been no crucifixion. Sometimes we have to face a sort of crucifixion before we can rise again and face the future. There's an old saying, author unknown, that goes like this: I am down, but I am not slain. I'll lay me down and bleed a while, then I'll rise and fight again.*

Was Tom imagining things, or did the minister look directly at him when he said these things? He thought about the way he had been told to get out after his wife had challenged him for his unfaithfulness. What a fool he had been. But it was not he who had been crucified as a result of his behaviour. It was his wife. She was the one bleeding. He was the crucifier. The realization stunned him.

It had happened at a medical conference on diabetes. He had invited his young practice nurse to join him because she had responsibilities that brought her into contact with his diabetic patients. But, after a few drinks one evening, one thing had led to another. His wife would never have known but someone at the conference had sent a letter to Mary. It was of the poison-pen variety, telling her that her husband was fooling around with someone nearly half his age. Details were supplied. Tom never quite worked out how anyone at the conference knew the details, but he had a vague recollection of misbehaving with Lucy in the bar before they went upstairs to bed.

> *We pray 'lead us not into temptation' but it is all around us. Was Jesus tempted by Mary Magdalene? There are writers who would have us believe they had an affair, had a son, and fled to France. It's rubbish, of course, but, unsurprisingly, it has sold a great many books*

> *and got the media ever so excited. In laughing the idea to scorn, let's not fall into the trap of thinking that Jesus did not experience the sort of temptations we face. The letter to the Hebrews in the New Testament tells us that Jesus was not someone untouched by the sort of weaknesses that challenge us. He was, says the letter, 'in all points tempted like as we are, but without sin.'*

Tom wondered why he had been such a fool as to give way to temptation. Lucy was half his age, a real bobby-dazzler and, as he discovered at the conference, without commitments and ready for a good time. Fatally, she told Tom she greatly admired him as a doctor loved and respected by his patients, and – this was especially appealing - because he looked much younger than his age. With his ego thus fed, he allowed himself to be steered into Lucy's room when they went upstairs to bed.

> *Jesus was without sin but, as for you and me, we certainly are not. As scripture says we have all fallen short. What's your latest disaster; your most recent failure to live up to the standards that you like people to believe you set yourself; your moral collapse in face of temptation? How are you going to deal with that? I will tell you what to do, assuming you are sorry.*

Tom's attention was now total. Never mind counting the organ pipes, or making up words from the names of the war dead on the wall. He had done that a few times in the past when he was bored. Mary, who was usually in church with him, had told him off for that. Having stormed at him for something much more serious, she could not face attending church, even on Easter Day. Tom, now crouched with total attentiveness in his pew, waited to hear the minister's prescription for healing the massive wound he had inflicted on his wife.

> *What you have to do is very, very simple, but also calls for courage. When Saint Peter preached the Easter message to the people at Pentecost, they asked, deeply affected: 'What shall we do?' My friends, is anyone among you this morning asking that question? Here's the answer Peter gave, and I give it to you this Easter Day: 'Repent'. Are you repentant? Have you committed some grievous sin that has broken someone's heart? Repent. Now. In this holy place. On this holiest of days.*

Tom was no longer crouching. He was on his knees, with tears in his eyes. 'I do, I do, I do. God forgive me. God help me.' In his distress, he could not suppress his emotions. His words could be clearly heard by others. They were heard by the man in the pulpit. 'Look', he said, 'our Tom is on his knees. Who else ought to be?' His words rang out across the church. 'Come on,' he declared, 'this is the chance of a lifetime for anyone here who is prepared to repent anything they have done of which they are ashamed. Come forward and kneel at the communion rail.' Tom, in great distress, summoning all his courage in a place where he was regarded as an upstanding member of the local community, led the way. After placing his hands on the seven heads that were bowed at the rail and declaring God's forgiveness of them, the minister remounted the pulpit as the supplicants returned to their seats.

*I haven't finished. Did you think I had? Oh, no. You who have received God's forgiveness have more to do. The Easter story gives us a clue. Think of St Luke's riveting account of Jesus walking to Emmaus with two travellers on the evening of the first Easter Day. They invited him to stay with them and realized who he was when he broke and blessed the bread. Then what did they do? Here it is: 'They rose that same hour and returned to Jerusalem and told what had happened on the road, and how Jesus was known to them in the breaking of bread.' They had to share their experience. So must you. If this morning has been for you a moment of repentance, go*

> *now to those you have hurt and make known to them what has happened to you. As God has forgiven you, so may they, and healing will begin.*

So it was that Tom and Mary's marriage was rescued from disaster. On Easter Monday, it being a bank holiday, Tom and Mary went walking in the Derbyshire peak district, which they had often done before they were married, and still loved to do. Climbing up Cubar Edge and looking out together across the glorious landscape, Tom said, 'Remember the day we got soaked up here? People thought we were a couple of mad teenagers.' There was silence, then Mary quietly replied: 'We were. We were madly in love. We didn't care about the rain. We were together and happy.' They held one another. Healing had begun.

# IN MEMORIAM

*On a cliff overlooking the sea at Winspit, near Swanage, there is a memorial plaque which names Ian Campbell Johnstone as having drowned there on 19th August 1935 at the age of 18. Below this information, these lines appear:*

> *He loved birds and green places*
> *And the wind on the heath*
> *And saw the brightness of the skirts of God*

*The present author's thoughts about that memorial gave rise to the story that follows.*

David Jackson, born 1971, a brilliant young violinist and ambitious climber of mountains, died at 28, as the twenty-first century was about to begin. During his short life, music and mountains preoccupied him. His ideal day was one in which he did some climbing then, in the evening, listened to the music of Mendelssohn. Once, roped together with him on a rugged Scottish mountain that seemed to rise vertically from the sea to touch the clouds, Dick Bridges said, shouting against the wind: 'I suppose we'll be listening to 'Fingal's Cave' tonight. I don't think I can stand it.' 'That's because', shouted David, 'underneath your tough exterior there lies a heart of stone.'

Neither David's parents nor his fellow musicians understood his obsession with the music of Felix Mendelssohn, but there was no doubting the young man's understanding of the great man's work. His playing of the violin concerto in E at the Royal Festival Hall earned rave reviews from the critics. 'David Jackson', wrote one critic, 'still in his early twenties, played as if he had sat with the composer and worked with him in creating the concerto. His playing of Mendelssohn's music almost makes me believe in reincarnation.'

* * *

In 1829, when he was twenty, Felix Mendelssohn set out from his home in Germany to explore Scotland with his friend Karl Klingemann. He was hugely excited by its craggy mountains and roaring seas. The sounds of the wind and waves on rocky shores stirred his imagination. Looking westwards, after climbing Ben More on Mull, he told Karl: 'We must go out to those islands between here and Tiree. I want to see Fingal's Cave on Staffa.'

Taken by boat to that tiny island, Mendelssohn was spellbound, as John Keats had been ten years earlier, when he likened it to a cathedral. Karl pronounced the place hideous and frightening, but Felix could not be drawn away. The black and purple columns that stood sentry at the cavern's mouth as the sea crashed and foamed around them seemed like mighty organ pipes, sending thunderous music into the air above the glistening spray. Felix said: 'I can capture this wild and magnificent place.' Within days, he had sent to his devoted sister Fanny the opening theme of what was to become 'The Hebrides Overture'.

Two years later, Felix and Karl were once again exploring territory new to them, this time in Switzerland. Looking out from the Jungfrau northwards, towards the Eiger and Interlaken, Felix said: 'This is a truly beautiful country. It's where I want to live if I grow very old.' 'What do you mean, *if*', responded his friend, 'you've not got yourself in some kind of fix, have you? You've not been drawn into this ridiculous duelling the Prussians are so keen on? It's crazy.' Felix laughed. 'No such thing. I've got so much music inside my head trying to get out that it wears me out. I'll die of exhaustion!'

After Switzerland, Felix spent the winter of his twenty-second year in Paris. With the collapse of the Bourbon monarchy the previous year, France was in celebratory mood. In the French capital, those of artistic temperament gave free rein to their way of life. Felix wrote home to Fanny that he had heard

Franz Liszt play the piano and Niccolo Paganini the violin. 'That Paganini', said Felix, 'plays the violin like no one I've ever heard before. But why the dark glasses?' 'He's a comedian. He does it for fun. You should see him at a party. He's the life and soul', replied Karl.

* * *

Charles Jackson, David's father, said: 'We must get away and try to forget.' 'I don't want to forget', replied his wife, 'I want to remember. Even if it hurts, I want to remember.' 'Yes, you're right, of course', her husband replied, 'we must remember.' He was silent for a while, then said, 'Let's go to Switzerland. He always hoped to climb there one day, like his cynosure, Felix Mendelssohn'. 'I do not know that word', said Helen Jackson. 'A cynosure shines brightly', said Charles, a retired teacher and inclined to used unfamiliar words to impress. He continued: 'The pole star is a cynosure. We look up to it.' Helen thought about that, then declared, 'Oh yes, I see. You're talking about David and his obsession with Mendelssohn. Yes, let's go to Switzerland. It might help us to feel close to him. I dreamt about him again last night.'

Not long after, their coach swept into Interlaken. 'Look', said Helen, 'there's the Eiger. Did Mendelssohn climb that?' 'No', said Charles, 'he went up the

Jungfrau. It's the next peak and its higher.' He paused, then added, 'I read somewhere that he fell in love with Switzerland that day and said he'd like to grow old and die here.'

The coach disgorged its party at the hotel where they were to stay. Charles was first at the check-in desk, as he had been in climbing aboard the coach that morning in Berne. He used to tell young teachers: 'Get to the classroom first, then you are in control.' He fidgeted anxiously as his wife changed for dinner, examining his watch every couple of minutes. 'We want a decent table', he said, 'and we must avoid sitting with those Jenkins people.'

John and Carol Jenkins rather liked the Jacksons and quickly made their way to the two empty seats at their table. 'Hullo again', said John, 'may we join you? In Berne, we heard you talking about Interlaken and it seems that you know it.' 'No, we've never been here before', said Helen. Charles thought to himself that, though that be true, the reason they had come gave it a special place in their hearts. He felt Helen squeeze his hand under the table. It was her customary don't-say-anything signal. 'Some say the best view to be had of Switzerland is from the Jungfrau', said John Jenkins. 'Mendelssohn would have agreed.' Charles replied, 'he climbed it more than a hundred years ago as a young man. We're told it's not a particularly difficult climb. They say there's not much risk. No swirling oceans below.'

He felt his wife tremble slightly beside him and changed the subject to something safer: 'Are you interested in wild flowers?' 'I'm keen to find some eidelweiss', said Carol Jenkins. The conversation turned to the safe haven of Swiss flora.

* * *

By the time he was thirty-eight, Felix Mendelssohn was director of music at the Gewandhaus, Liepzig's prestigious concert centre. At his birthday party, he was persuaded to take part in a hilarious charade based on the name of the place, which means clothing hall. 'I hope', he said, 'this won't be the end of my reputation as a serious musician.' 'Unlikely', came the reply from his friend Karl Klingemann, 'it's Wagner you want to watch out for if you want to guard your reputation. He's jealous of you. Did you see what he said when you both conducted in Dresden?' Karl took a cutting from his pocket and read out Wagner's appraisal: 'My own simple and heartfelt composition entirely eclipsed the romantic artificialities of Mendelssohn.' But Felix was not going to be depressed on his birthday. 'That was five years ago. Wagner has said kinder things since.'

Despite the festive mood, Felix was not well. 'I feel weary all the time', he told Karl, 'and these constant headaches are getting me down.' Karl had been worried for some time, watching his friend's increasingly grey pallor and sunken eyes. He had passed on his concerns to Cecile, the musician's deeply caring wife. 'He looks old well beyond his years', he had said. Cecile resolved to take her husband on holiday. Where would it be best to go? 'Switzerland', insisted Felix. Later, Cecile wondered if he had some inkling of a premature death. Had he not once said that he would want be there at the end of his life? At Interlaken, Felix took long walks on his own along the shores of the lake. He called at the little churches nestling here and there, playing the organ in some of them. Cecile watched and hoped.

Returning to Germany, Felix was unable to face the public. Engaged to conduct the first German performance of his *Elijah* in Berlin, he could not face it and the event was cancelled. Back in Leipzig, he became dull and listless. Asked how he felt, his answer was always the same: 'Tired and grey, tired and grey.' As the year in which he had celebrated his thirty-eighth birthday drew to a close, Felix Mendelssohn's life did the same.

In due course, a splendid statue of him by the sculptor Erwin Stein was placed outside the Gewandhaus in Leipzig, but it was destroyed in 1936 on the orders of the mayor of the city at the bidding of Nazi headquarters in Berlin. Shortly afterwards, Sir Thomas Beecham came with the London Philharmonic Orchestra and was surprised not to see the statue of Leipzig's most famous composer. On returning home, Sir Thomas said: 'I think the Nazis have smashed Mendelssohn's statute. Their attitude to Jews is a disgrace. But his music will be played long after their power and influence have bitten the dust. That is his memorial.'

* * *

Charles Jackson recalled an occasion when his son David had said: 'You know, if I'm going to die young, I want it to happen when I am doing something wonderful, like attempting some impossible climb.' He laughed as he said it but his mother told him not to talk like that. She remembered the conversation now, as she and her husband reached the foothills of the Jungfrau and looked up towards the peak, standing sharp and clear in the morning sunshine against a cloudless sky. 'David would have loved it here', she said. 'Yes', her husband responded, 'I guess he would have been of the same mind as Mendelssohn. Perhaps they talk together about climbing, and about music, wherever they are now, beyond all this.'

The couple were silent. Their heads raised towards the mountain, the scent of the wild flowers on its lower slopes filling their nostrils. There was little or no wind at this level and the sense of quiet peacefulness was overwhelming. The woman felt as if time, and her physicality, were suspended. There was a gentle stir in the air beside her and she felt her son's comforting nearness. Her husband began to move away towards Grindenwald and she followed him along the descending hillside path. After awhile, reluctant to return to reality, she said, 'Let's rest.' The couple sat together on a flat stone beside a brook. Helen made to speak, then hesitated, reluctant to share her experience for fear that its magic might be dispelled. 'David was there', she said, 'I felt him close, so very close.' There was a long silence. Charles said, 'Yes, I know. I felt his presence too. It was right that we came.' They clung to one another.

After a while, they climbed to their feet and wandered downwards into the countryside beside the lake, which shimmered in the sunlight. They came by chance to a small chapel, nestling beside a bridge over a fast-flowing stream. In the following days, Charles and Helen would ask one another whether they had come to that place other than by chance. Within the chapel, there was a plaque commemorating a visit by Felix Mendelssohn. They went outside and saw a woman tending a nearby bank covered in wild flowers. She beckoned them over, realizing they were visitors. 'Look', she said, 'here is eidelweiss.' Thinking she must be a gardener, Charles asked her how often she came to tend the chapel grounds. 'I spend one day a week in this corner to keep it nice for my son. See, here is his grave.' It lay below the flowered bank.

The woman had not beckoned the couple over to see the edelweiss. She had a deeper purpose, which was to relate her story. It always helped her to do so. 'My Michael', she said, 'fell on the Jungfrau two years ago. It was a Tuesday, which is the day I always come here. Sometimes my husband and I think our son's spirit is still up there on the mountain. Sometimes we go and lay flowers in the foothills. We are sure Michael comes near to comfort us.'

The woman was not sad. She seemed at peace with her memories of her son. She smiled. 'You must perhaps excuse me for telling you this story, but it is good that we talk to one another of those we love and see no more. Otherwise, the hurting goes on and on. To share is to help the healing come.' Some lines Charles had written secretly, just for himself, at the time of David's fatal fall from a cliff face, to express his agony, came to his mind:

> The echoing anguish of the gulls gives voice
>     to the pain I cannot bear;
> From the melancholy cliff top comes the
>     music of despair.

Helen Jackson said to the woman at the graveside: 'We lost our son, as you did yours. He was climbing in Scotland, in what we call the Hebrides. He fell from a cliff into the sea. He was never found.' She paused. The woman waited, sensing that there was something more to be said. 'There is no grave for us to tend', said Helen. The woman gently shook her head. She said, 'It must not be so. You must find a place. You must go and look down on the sea where your son made his grave. You will find his spirit there.'

Passing through the chapel and making their way to the main door which would lead them to the little bridge they had crossed earlier, they realized that the sound of the tumbling stream could be clearly heard from inside the building. The woman had followed them and said, 'You hear the water? That is good. Our pastor tells us that it is God's way of reminding us that his providence is poured out upon us whenever we are in need.' She smiled, adding, 'Return to the place where your son fell. He is waiting.'

On a Hebridean cliff overlooking the Atlantic Ocean there is a plaque set in a rock. It bears this inscription:

**DAVID CHARLES JACKSON 1971–1999**

**He loved the wind in his hair and the open sky above him, the wheeling gulls and the sea on the rocks, the climb upwards and the music of Mendelssohn at the day's close. May his violin echo in the cathedrals of heaven.**

Once a year, an ageing couple come and lay flowers beside the plaque. Then they hold hands and look down upon the tumbling waves that spit and foam against the rocks below. Sometimes the wind roars so loudly that little else can be heard, but when it moderates and whispers sibilantly in crevices, one might imagine the sound of a violin.

# DUGGIE

The Crookback Club was not listed in the school magazine. Its activities were not of that kind. It was Duggie who thought it up during a history lesson. He had never been any good at school work except for art, but he sometimes gave history a bit of attention as it was a subject in which there was quite often a bit of violence. There was this lesson when they heard about Julia Caesar getting knifed by Brutals. Julia was in fact a man, though he had a woman's name. Duggie assumed he was queer, so he deserved what he got.

In one history lesson they did about a king named Richard who had two kids murdered to get the throne. He had a nickname, Richard Crookback, because he was born with a hump. He knew people talked about his deformed body. It filled him with hate and made him want to get his own back on life. Duggie understood. He had been called Twistgob because he had a cleft palate. He put a stop to that with his fists and boots, but his fury at having a deformity seethed inside him.

Having a smoke behind the pavilion one morning

break, Duggie said, in his strange nasal voice, 'I can't wait to finish with this place. Miss Crane is the only teacher who has ever said anything good about me.' He had just been told off for wearing his big boots to school by a teacher he didn't even know. Tyrone, who had leadership qualities unrecognized by those who attempted to teach him, said, 'We ought to put the knife into some of them here.' The others waited. Tyrone often kept his best ideas for last. He said, 'After that we should torch the place.'

There were five of them at the pavilion. While Duggie was overweight, Tyrone was tall and muscular. His black hair, permanent scowl and thin lips gave him a threatening air. Some of the staff found him frightening. Those just out of college were warned: 'Try not to get on the wrong side of Tyrone Matthews.' Young women were advised to be wary of finding themselves alone with him. His parents had given up trying to exercise any control over him, despite realising that some of the things in his bedroom must have been stolen.

Then there were the Barton twins, Jake and Rick. As first glance, they appeared a couple of perfectly ordinary teenage boys, only distinguishable from one another by a scar over Jake's left eye, put there by one of his mother's passing boy friends, a tall man, but morbidly fat. He got the worst of it in arguing with Jake and going for him. In doing so, he had to face his twin brother at the same time, a development of which he had not taken account. He was no match for the Bartons with their knuckle dusters. When anyone dared to refer to Jake's scar, they got the traditional answer, expressed in a most sinister manner: 'You should see the other bloke.'

The brothers were slim, wiry characters with fair hair and piercing blue eyes that looked out on the world with cold hostility. On Saturdays they looked forward to attacking visiting supporters when Millwall were at home. They liked to travel to away games and start trouble on the terraces. If they went by train, they did not bother to buy tickets. No ticket inspector who had heard of the Bartons was going to confront them and demand that they pay.

The only girl in the group was Mandy. Cleaned up and properly dressed, she would have presented as slim and attractive, but everything about her expressed her defiance of authority. A not-very-clean white blouse spilled out of a tight black skirt which she had rolled over at the waist so that the hemline came halfway up her thighs. Her hair was lank and her fingers stained with nicotine. Her shoes were filthy. She did not smell very good. She had been in care since the age of thirteen when her mother abandoned her four children to go off with a long-distance lorry driver. Mandy's response to every mishap and humiliation in her life was: 'Don't care.'

Geraint Jones was newly appointed to teach French, having previously been on the staff of a further education college that was phasing out its languages department. He found the pupils of the school difficult to handle. After his first confrontation with Mandy, he gave his frank verdict in the staffroom. 'What an awful girl', he declared. 'Why is she allowed to get away with looking so disgusting and behaving like a harlot.' Grace Fleming, the immaculate head of domestic science, who had previously taught in a small girls' grammar school, suggested to the headmaster that he should write to that girl Mandy White's parents about her disgraceful appearance. 'Mandy White hasn't got any parents', came the reply. 'To tell the truth', said John Grainger, 'Mandy has never had any of the things a girl is entitled to, such as a little love and understanding.' Grace walked away. She had realized soon after he arrived that John Grainger was weak on discipline.

All five miscreants cut school the day after Duggie was told off about his boots. They met as usual under the railway bridge. The police came round there from time to time, asking questions in a just-wanting-a-friendly-chat kind of way when there had been trouble in the town. The five were never moved on or asked why they weren't in school. Mandy had it from a mate who knew a copper that the police liked to know where to find her and her associates. Just to keep the filth happy, Tyrone or the Bartons would point them in the direction of other trouble-makers now and again. They didn't mind putting the boot in on other miscreants. It was a laugh.

Duggie leaned back against the graffiti-covered wall of the bridge. He said, 'If we're going to carve up a few people, we need an identity.' 'Yer what?', said Jake. 'I'm not going in no identity parade!', said his twin. Tyrone said, 'I was in one, but they never nailed me. Some other bloke got fingered for what I done. The fuzz went spare.'

Duggie said, 'No, I'm not talking about anything like that. Remember when Clink said in history about them that went round smashing machines? They had a name.' 'What was it?', asked Tyrone. 'Dunno', said Duggie, 'Clink told us but I weren't listening by them. I'd dropped something to look up Suzie Naylor's skirt.' Clink Hunter, so called because his ill-fitting false teeth sometimes rattled when he spoke, didn't notice what Duggie was up to. After thirty years in the classroom, he didn't notice very much at all. It meant he didn't have to do anything about what was going on that shouldn't be.

Duggie was getting annoyed. He said, 'If you were one of them that smashed the machines, who were called something, you were somebody. You got in the history books. It's like them gangs in West Side Story.' The others suddenly showed an interest. They all knew about the Jets and the Sharks. Duggie said, 'Remember that bloke with a hump in his back who knifed a couple of kids? Clink told us they called him Crookback. Why don't we call ourselves the Crookback Club? I bet nobody would tumble.' 'Clever', said Mandy. Duggie felt good. Nobody except Miss Crane said anything like that about him. 'Let's just be the Crookbacks', said Rick, and it was agreed.

'We need a target', said Tyrone, 'Let's start with an easy one. Let's wipe the smile off the face of that bossy prefect, Robinson.' The suggestion was welcomed with hoots of approval. Tyrone went on. 'Duggie', he said, 'this was your idea. How about having first go?' Duggie felt even better. To be thought clever by Mandy was great; to be acknowledged by someone like Ty was huge.

Knifing Robinson, thought Duggie, would be better than almost anything that had happened to him since coming to the school, except for his art lessons. It would be better than passing exams, better even than going up on the platform to get a prize in front of everybody. Robinson pushed people around when he thought they didn't amount to much. Duggie knew he himself was no great thinker but he was sure that the whole world would be better off without people of the Robinson kind. Maybe he was right. Ty said, 'When it's done, we have to let it be known that it was the Crookbacks that done it.' Jake said, 'I'll write on a blackboard somewhere. The word will get round.'

The injury to Dale Robinson of the lower sixth when he was knifed in the side during the bustle in the corridors at change of lessons caused a sensation. While everyone was wondering who had wounded Dale, someone wrote on a blackboard in large letters: THE CROOKBACKS DONE IT. Taken by ambulance to hospital for attention to a relatively minor wound, there was found in one of the victim's pockets a quantity of cannabis. The attack, concluded the police, was clearly drugs related. Dale Robinson was not the good citizen some had assumed. George Evans, head of history, a peppery little man with a piping voice, declared: 'I never did like that boy. Too full of himself. A bit of a Flashman. Very dodgy. Should never have been made a prefect.' George had not recovered from an occasion when Robinson had barged into him in the corridor and failed to apologise and call him 'Sir' when reprimanded. The boy's descent into criminal activity probably began then.

The identity of Dale Robinson's attacker was never discovered. Interest in the drugs aspect predominated. The local press had a field day, assisted by disgruntled parents who had never wanted their offspring to attend the school. 'We always knew it was a bog-standard place,' said one disgruntled mother, 'our Sarah only went there because we were refused our first two choices.'

A picture appeared on the front page of the local paper showing a group of boys smoking on their way to school. A reporter had given them the cigarettes. They didn't contain cannabis, but you couldn't tell. The headline read: GOING TO POT. There was a further picture of a group of teenagers huddled behind a gymnasium. They hadn't realized they were being photographed. The editor of the paper was delighted with it. The report that went with it advanced the possibility that the knifing incident was part of warfare between rival gangs trading in illegal substances.

John Grainger, the headmaster, remained cool. That surprised the local authority's school inspector, who said he would be coming to the school. 'By all means', sighed John Grainger, 'but don't get too excited. There's no truth in the story and it will soon blow over when the media sniff out some disaster in another school.' The inspector was unsettled by this. He had been head of a distinguished grammar school and his media experience was limited to reporting impressive examination results and inviting the local press to take photographs of successful Oxbridge candidates. To his inspectorate colleagues he had once claimed that he had never in his life come across young people like some of those at the comprehensive for which he was responsible. His appointment owed a good deal to the hope at county hall that he would turn the place into something like a grammar school.

John Grainger's meeting with the inspector was unsatisfactory. He said, 'We do now and again find a boy or girl in possession of cannabis. It happens in many schools, including this country's top public schools. We normally suspend the offender and call the parents in. We've had three cases this school year, two of them involving twin boys who were caught smoking pot behind the pavilion. Suspension was no new experience for them and only mother turned up. She told us, not for the first time, that the boys' father was the only one who could control 'them two buggers', but he was away. The school knew he was in fact serving a sentence for armed robbery. 'Good heavens', said the inspector, 'what on earth can be done for lads from such homes?' 'Not a lot', said John Grainger mournfully, 'While they are here we do our best to let them know we care what happens to them, but I won't pretend all the staff take that view.'

The headmaster thought of the occasion when he was interviewed on the radio on the subject of school discipline when corporal punishment was exciting the interest of the media. The interviewer, with a slip of the tongue, had asked, 'What is your view about capital punishment for those who misbehave?' John Grainger, unable to resist the temptation, had said, 'Well, I can think of a few I would have liked to hang, but we haven't come to that yet.' He got into trouble with his governors for saying that, but it had given his friends in the profession a laugh.

He brought his attention back to his discussion with the inspector. He said, 'Some of our hard cases are due to leave school soon. God help the poor social services. It's the way of the world, I'm afraid.' He went on to express his view that some children were born to parents quite unfit to raise them. 'Hm', said the inspector uneasily, 'you sound as if you agree with what Keith Joseph said back in 1974.' John Grainger took a deep breath and responded. He had a reputation for being controversial. He said, 'Well, I had a letter published in *The Times* when that furore took place, stating that the Minister had raised an important issue. He'd been clobbered by the media for sounding in favour of selective breeding, like Adolf Hitler. He sent me a personal letter thanking me. He had obviously been deeply hurt by the things people were saying about him. A strange man. I don't know how he ever got into politics. The *Times*

*Educational Supplement* always referred to him as the Mad Monk.'*

John Grainger realized he was going on a bit and stopped talking. The inspector said, 'You know, John, it's no surprise to me that the people at county hall say you like to live dangerously. Why on earth do you make yourself so vulnerable?' The invitation was irresistible. 'Look', said John Grainger, 'we have in this school a small number of pupils who cause enormous problems. They require a great deal of time and attention to minimize their disruptive influence. They have no interest in education.' His voice rose. 'Their ambition is to prevent any taking place! It only takes one or two bent on disorder to make it impossible to teach the rest. It's no good trying to get their parents involved. They gave up on their kids long ago. They probably had a bad experience of school themselves. The cycle

* Keith Joseph, Secretary of State for Social Services, made a statement in 1974 that ended his prospects of the Conservative Party leadership when he observed:

> The balance of our population, our human stock, is threatened. A high and rising proportion of children are being born to mothers least fitted to bring children into the world. Some are of low intelligence, most of low educational attainment. They are unlikely to be able to give children the stable emotional background, the consistent combination of love and fitness, which are more important than riches. They are producing problem children. Yet these mothers, the under-twenties in many cases, single parents, from classes four to five, are now producing a third of all births.
>
> Source: AN Wilson, *Our Times 1953–2008*, Hutchinson, 2008.

of failure and delinquency is passed on from one generation to the next.' He paused, then delivered a discouraging prophecy: 'There are teenagers here who will come to a nasty end and there's not a lot we can do to prevent it.' Little did he know how prescient that statement would prove.

Some of the young people the headmaster had in mind were not in school that day. They were gathered under the railway bridge, celebrating the trouble they had caused and plotting their next move. Tyrone said, 'We ought to do Jackson next.' 'No', responded Mandy, 'I say it ought to be a woman. I'd like to slip a knife into that deputy head.' Linda Clough, the person under consideration, had many a run-in with Mandy White. What really made the girl seethe was her suspicion that Miss Clough wanted to help her. She could do without some do-gooder trying to sort her out. Stuff that.

Duggie thought the deputy head wouldn't be as easy to do as Robinson had been. 'Leave her to me', said Mandy menacingly. With one eye closed because tobacco smoke was drifting up from the side of her mouth, and with her provocative version of school uniform, she looked anything but a schoolgirl. Bill Denby, head of the fifth year, thought she could look attractive with a little effort. 'Like Eliza Doolittle', he said, 'she would scrub up very well.' 'Actually', responded Linda Clough, soon to be knifed by Mandy, 'she might make something of herself if she wasn't so full of hate. It's not her fault. Her home is a battlefield, poor kid.'

The murder of Linda Clough caught the late evening news on television on the Friday when it happened. The police were saying no more than that she had been attacked in the school car park. As usual for her, she was the last to leave the premises and her attacker had stabbed her in the back as she was putting an armful of papers in the boot of her car. There were no witnesses. Her body, sprawled on the tarmac, was discovered by one of the school cleaners who arrived an hour after the event.

In assembly on Monday morning, the headmaster paid tribute to Miss Clough and asked everyone to bow their heads for two minutes of silence in her honour. Mandy looked sideways at Rick and winked. John Grainger said: 'Police will be investigating this dreadful crime. The guilty party will be found out. Meanwhile, please remain calm. Please do not gossip about this incident. Lessons will proceed as usual.'

After assembly, the school keeper asked to see the head. This was most unusual. George Acland, an ex-naval chief petty officer, ran his side of things at the school with military efficiency, exercising unquestioned authority over his forty-plus school-keeping staff, and such teachers and pupils as he came across. Several teachers were more frightened of the school keeper than their classes were of them.

'Something's up', said Alan Beccles, the second deputy, when he learned that George Acland had requested a meeting, 'Shall I join you?'

The school keeper rapped smartly on the headmaster's door and entered the room. He was tall, well-built and immaculately groomed. It was easy to visualize him on the prow of a ship, his sharp blue eyes fixed on the horizon. He said, 'Headmaster, something is going on. A blackboard was taken from a classroom on Friday and one of my men found it on Saturday morning, propped against the wall of the car park. There was writing on it. Let me show you.' He turned and opened the door. A member of his staff entered on cue, holding a blackboard before him. A message had been chalked on it in capital letters: THE CROOKBACKS DONE IT. Alan Beccles said, 'Done what? Pinched a blackboard? That's no big deal!' John Grainger had inherited the second deputy from his predecessor and had never thought much of his perceptivity. Ignoring him and addressing the head, the school keeper said, 'The thing is, we found the same message on a blackboard when that prefect was knifed.' 'Thank you, Mr Acland,' replied the head, 'You were right to bring this to me. I just wonder why the police didn't spot it.' 'Well, headmaster', responded ex-chief petty office Acland, a man with a reputation during his time in the navy of missing nothing, 'I wondered about that too. Perhaps the police saw it but didn't make a connection with the crime. Some of them aren't too bright.' A bit like some teachers, he thought, eyeing Beccles.

Over the weekend, Mandy and the others met under the bridge. 'Hey, Mand', said Tyrone, 'we wasn't going to kill anybody'. Jake Barton said, 'Our dad reckons it's OK to duff someone up, but be careful. He says a good hiding is one thing but stiffing somebody can mean real trouble with the filth.' Jake and his brother didn't see much of their father because he was often detained at Her Majesty's pleasure, but they admired his exploits. Mandy was untroubled by what Jake had said. Her response was delivered with relish: 'I never meant to kill the bitch, but she had it coming. It felt real good, sticking the knife in her. It went in real deep. Lovely.'

Duggie said, 'What we been doing to get our own back on that school has turned out real easy. Nobody's got a sniff of what we're up to. Let's not hang about any more. Let's do what Ty said. You know, torch the place. We could put a notice on the gate after, saying we done it.' Mandy said, 'Great idea.' For a second time, she had made Duggie feel good.

The group began to plan an act of arson. The speed at which their deep hostility to the school moved on from knifing people to incendiarism was remarkable. Their early success convinced them that they were clever enough to get away with anything. Rick and Jake's father once warned them against being too sure of themselves. 'That's what got me banged up', he said. Remembering that, Rick Barton insisted that, if their next target was the school building, careful planning was necessary. They would need to set fires in several parts if the place was to be completely gutted.

Each of the five Crookbacks was allocated a different area and took responsibility for starting a fire there. Tyrone undertook to make some petrol bombs. His uncle Frank, who lived in Belfast, had once boasted of how easy it was and explained how to do it. Over a period of a fortnight, Tyrone went to five different garages and bought a can of petrol at each one, claiming that it was for his father's motor bike. He lifted a large box of cotton wool from a chemist shop and a crate of empty milk bottles from the yard at the dairy near his home. Finally, he went to a shop that sold fireworks all the year round, inquired about the largest matches they had in stock and bought a box. He took the materials he had assembled to a disused building on an overgrown plot of land and made five explosives. He put them in the milk crate and hid it under the bridge. When he got home, he dashed straight upstairs and shut himself in the bathroom to get the smell of petrol off his hands. His mother was surprised at his sudden enthusiasm for cleanliness but said nothing.

The five intending arsonists were full of nervous excitement as they broke into the school one Sunday night. As they had done before when searching for money, they got in through one of the ground floor windows. The school was due to be equipped with a system of burglar alarms, but the work had not yet been done.

Four of the group ignited their bombs in rooms on the ground, first, second and third floors. Mandy had claimed the sixth floor, where science was taught. In the planning session the previous day, she had said: 'I'm going to turn that science department into a bloody inferno. That moron Jackson told me I wasn't fit to be in his science class. He told me I looked like a tart and smelled worse than some of his chemicals. I'll show the bastard. He won't have no place to teach when I've done with the science block.' Tyrone had explained how he had fed the petrol-soaked cotton wool fuses into the bottles. He had made them long enough to give time for those lighting them to get away before the intended explosions, which would scatter burning petrol to set fire to anything inflammable nearby.

Duggie put his in a ground floor cloakroom, then went upstairs, intending to join the others. On the first floor, at a junction of corridors where the art department created displays of work, he stopped in his tracks. Before him stood a sculpture he had made. Miss Crane had told him it was amazing. She told his form teacher, Roger Lingard, that he ought to come and see it, but he never found time. She had even put a note in the box outside the headmaster's study telling him that Douglas Jenkins of 5RL had produced a piece of work of amazing power, but the piece of paper had got buried in a cascade of much more important documents and had never been read.

The work was a half-sized depiction of a man in chains. He had collapsed on the ground after struggling against his bonds. The soft clay had been moulded with astonishing skill. The face was delineated with a potter's knife with such sensitivity that the subject's aching despair leapt out at an onlooker. There were pearls of sweat on the face and neck. One chained hand was curled into a fist being shaken in anger against the world. Duggie had poured all his personal anguish into the work. Created in clay, it had been fired in the new giant kiln Julie Crane had persuaded the school to buy. She had told a colleague, 'If nothing else ever goes in there, it's been worth getting it.' Beside the work, the artist was named: Douglas Jenkins 5RL.

Susan Bridge, a young English teacher just out of college, had seen the figure on her way round the school in her first week. She had been dumbstruck. As she stood with another teacher, she said that it must surely be by that sixth former who was going to the Slade School of Art. 'Maybe', came the reply, 'but I don't think his name is Jenkins.'

The smell of smoke was beginning to pervade the building, but Duggie had lost interest in the arson project. He grabbed the chained figure, headed downstairs to the window by which the five had climbed in, carefully lowered his pottery sculpture on to the terrace outside the window, then clambered out dangerously near to the conflagration he had started, and made his escape.

After he and the Bartons had started fires on their designated floors, Tyrone said they should go and fetch Mandy from the top of the building, then get out fast. They raced up to the sixth level and found the girl laughing to herself with satisfaction. The glow of flames could be seen through the window of one laboratory door. 'This is bleeding great', she said. 'Time to scarper', said Tyrone. 'No', the girl insisted, 'I want to have a go at the lab technician's room. If I light a few of them big matches and chuck 'em in there, the chemicals will blow up. They'll see it for miles!' The delay she insisted upon proved fatal. By the time the girl was ready to run for it, smoke was beginning to drift up the main stairwell from below. Suddenly, a sheet of flame shot up the stairs. 'Bugger this', said Jake, 'let's get out.' Tyrone led the way down to the fourth floor landing, but flames made the stairs below impassable. 'The lifts' said Jake, a note of panic in his voice. 'Yea, course', said his brother. He pressed the call button that summoned one of the giant lifts, each capable of holding thirty people, that moved staff and pupils between floors. Nobody asked where Duggie might be. Had he known that, he would have shrugged his shoulders resignedly. He knew nobody really cared about him much. As the others climbed into the lift, Mandy pointed to a notice on the lift wall. 'You're not supposed to use these if there's a fire', she said. Jake laughed. 'You're not supposed to do a lot of the things we do', he declared. They were all laughing about that as Tyrone pressed the button to take them to the ground floor.

No fewer than five fire engines and their crews attempted to control the flames licking out from different parts of the main school building. It took several hours to dowse the furnace the Crookbacks had created. In one of the lifts, stuck between the second and third floors, four bodies were found. They were burnt so badly as to make it impossible to identify them immediately. It looked as if they had tried desperately to claw the doors of the lift open, fighting one another as they did so.

Over the ensuing five years and a half years, John Grainger presided over the rebuilding of his school, and its re-opening, after which he was appointed to the inspectorate as a man of unrivalled experience in the field of comprehensive education. The appointing committee at county hall had discussed at length the suitability of a making a man who had his school burned down an inspector, but opinion swung in John Grainger's favour when one member, an eloquent and persuasive government adviser on education, argued that there was a need in the inspectorate for someone who had, in trying to run one of the massive comprehensives built by the local authority, faced enormous difficulties. 'For God's sake', said Aubrey Skevington-Wood, soon to become an MP, 'the man survived an arson attack, supervised the rebuilding of his school, and ended up with good examination results.' Aubrey had hopes of one day becoming an education minister and knew that examination results were what mattered most in assessing a school.

Meanwhile, Duggie Jenkins, sole surviving member of the Crookback gang, was making a name for himself in the art world. He had managed to get a part-time job filling shelves at a supermarket but, in the light of what his art teacher at school had said about him, he decided to join an art class at a local evening school. He had taken along the piece of work he had rescued from the flames as evidence of his ability. The teacher of the class turned out to be Roger Salmon, an influential member of the London art intelligentsia. One thing led to another and Duggie ended up at the Slade with a grant from Roger Salmon's foundation for young artists, the FYA. In due course, at an exhibition of his work,

Duggie sold no fewer than nine of his creations. Somewhat extravagantly, one of his teachers at the Slade had said: 'Henry Moore is yesterday. Douglas Jenkins is tomorrow.'

It was the story of Duggie's early years, and of his first interest in art, that captured the attention of the media. The tale of a boy who appeared to have failed at school but whose one great talent had been discovered there, saving him from a life of poverty and crime – he had got in with a bad lot at school – featured one day in a *Sunday Telegraph* piece when the usual stuff about falling standards in schools was in the news. A reporter had persuaded Duggie's mother to talk about her son.

Biddy Jenkins was a single mother. Duggie was her only child and she had done her best to bring him up proper, as she put it. She understood when he hurled abuse at her in his early teens over his facial deformity. 'Look at this', he had stormed, 'what am I ever going to amount to with a face like this.' A teacher who found him difficult to handle once told him: 'You'll never amount to anything. You're a loser.' He didn't really blame his mother. He actually cared a lot about her because he realized she hadn't had much luck either.

After he became newsworthy, Biddy acquired a new perspective on her son. She told the reporter he was a good boy who was always kind to his mum. She knew he would make good. She was able to recall his early artistic efforts as a toddler. 'He made some wonderful things with play dough', she said, 'then later with some clay he got from school.' Sadly, she was unable to show any of Duggie's infant or adolescent creations, despite offers of money from tabloids that followed up the *Sunday Telegraph* piece.

By the time he was thirty-five, Douglas Ray Jenkins, known simply as DRJ among those knowledgeable about art, was a wealthy man. He had extended the range of his creations well beyond what Julie Crane had brought about. He had a phenomenal appetite for work as he explored different materials. He produced bronze sculptures, exquisite wood carvings and multi-material structures. His life-sized depiction in polished steel of two sumo wrestlers stood in the lobby of the most expensive hotel in Tokyo.

DRJ's most famous piece was displayed at the Slade School of Art, where he had been a mature student. It was what one critic had described as 'an arresting, stunning, pulsating image of a man on the edge of despair.' Life-sized, the figure struggled to break free of chains that bound him, one clenched fist shaken at a heedless world. Cast in bronze, it had been said of the sculpture that it was a reminder to the whole world of the condition of those at the bottom of the social pile. The original was Duggie's most treasured possession.

'Ladies and gentlemen, governors of the school,

representatives of the local education authority, teachers and students, it is my great pleasure and privilege to introduce this evening one of our most distinguished former students.' The head teacher, Susan Bridge, had begun her career at the school in what were known as the BF days, before the fire. After great success as an English specialist, she became the head of department in the difficult days when the school was scattered in three temporary locations. She then left to get some experience elsewhere as deputy head of a comprehensive in Liverpool. Seeing the advertisement for the headship of her first school, which had been rebuilt, she excitedly applied for it, but without great hopes of success, thinking that the governors might not want someone running the place who would be a reminder of the disaster long ago.

She continued her speech of introduction. 'Our speaker this evening is a reminder that talent takes many forms. Yes, of course examination results matter, and we are proud of the school's academic achievements. But it is our responsibility to value all our young people, whatever they are like.' She paused to smile, then added, 'And that includes those who give us trouble. They matter too.' Duggie, sitting on the platform in a highly exposed position, kept a straight face but thought to himself: 'I wonder if there's still a gang here plotting to burn the place down?'

Duggie's appearance and manner had been transformed by his achievements. Expensive surgery had improved his facial features. The days of Twistgob were but a distant memory. His cleft palate could still be detected in the nasal tone of his speech, but it was not nearly as pronounced as had once been the case. He was expensively dressed in a manner he thought appropriate for a member of the artistic fraternity – he wore a maroon velvet jacket and brown corduroy trousers, both purchased in St James' Street. There was a silk cravat at his neck and tailor made shoes on his feet. He wore his hair long. Susan Bridge said, 'Ladies and gentlemen, students of this school, I am proud to present Mr Douglas Ray Jenkins.'

'I was a failure here', said Duggie, 'a truant and a trouble-maker. I knew the gang who burned the old school down.' There were audible gasps on the platform and round the hall. 'They were real hard cases. They played the teachers up something awful. I did, too.' He paused for effect. He had become good at making speeches. The last one had been to members of the Royal Society of Arts on the subject 'Using Art to Change the World.' He'd been treated like royalty at RSA headquarters in John Adam Street, hard by Charing Cross.

'Look at me now', he said. 'How come I've made good? A teacher saved my life. She showed me how to create a work of art and believed in me so I went and did it. That's what we all need – someone who believes in us. Miss Crane – that's who it was – taught me that I was good at something; that I was worth something; that I mattered.' Julie Crane, nearing retirement after what seemed a lifetime in the school, felt eyes upon her. She was not someone who was used to getting noticed. There were two local newspaper reporters in the audience and they both scribble down her name. She was about to become a local celebrity.

Looking across the assembled students, Duggie said, 'I tell you, if you've got teachers who show they believe in you, you'll never forget them.' He paused again, looking round the hall in the direction of teachers who sat against the walls. 'Let me say to you teachers', he said, 'you don't just teach a subject. You teach what you are. That means teaching is one of the most terrifying, the most demanding, the most exciting jobs there is. If you're any good at it, there are people walking round planet Earth who thank God for you. I thank God for my art teacher. I wouldn't be here if it wasn't for her.' Both the reporters wrote that down.

'Hey, you lot', declared Duggie to the assembled boys and girls, 'be kind to your teachers. They care about you more than you might think.' He thought that there were some who didn't care and who regarded those they were supposed to teach as their natural enemies, but he had better not go into that.

He went on, 'When I was here, I used to think how great it would be to come up on this platform and get a prize. Congratulations to all of you who have received prizes today. But if you haven't got one, and find your lessons difficult, don't worry. Out there in the real world, your day will come, if you believe in yourself. Everybody's good at something. Life's about finding out what.'

Duggie had now departed from what he had prepared and was saying just what came into his head. He was enjoying being the centre of attention. But he realized it was time for him to shut up so he said what his mum had brought him up to say when invited to a party as a small child: 'Thank you for having me.' He sat down to warm applause that lasted ninety-three seconds and broke the record kept by John Rhodes, a maths teacher, who ran a sweepstake every year on the length of applause received by the visiting speaker. The winner this time was Stuart Hill, a newcomer to the staff, who was bewildered by what Duggie had said. Was he really expected to care about that awful girl Sarah Bonds, who made his lessons hell? She looked like a tart and didn't smell very good. They hadn't warned him about pupils like her at training college. One of these days he would tell her just what he thought of her. That would sort her out.